THE SKY DIDN'T LOAD TODAY AND OTHER GLITCHES

THE SKY DIDN'T LOAD TODAY AND OTHER GLITCHES

RICH LARSON

FLAME ARROW PUBLISHING

PRAISE FOR RICH LARSON

"Larson demonstrates his superhuman ability to weld wild future-world concepts with immediately relatable characters. Upload this book into your mind at the fastest possible Mbps."

MIKE ALLEN, WORLD FANTASY AWARD-NOMINATED AUTHOR OF *UNSEAMING* AND *SLOW BURN*

"Startling and seductive…These stories are a virtuosic exploration of human striving in the face of existential collapse."

IAN MUNESHWAR, NEBULA, LOCUS, AND SHIRLEY JACKSON AWARD FINALIST

"Rich Larson is one of my very favorite short story writers, and his powers are undiminished in these haunting brilliant short-shorts, each one a deeply-felt world in miniature."

SAM J MILLER, NEBULA-AWARD-WINNING AUTHOR OF *BLACKFISH CITY*

"Effective flash fiction that leaves an impression... Rich Larson writes brilliantly at every length."

ELLEN DATLOW, MULTI-AWARD WINNING EDITOR OF SHORT FICTION

"Larson has a knack for fitting mind-bending ideas, interesting characters, and dark and compelling twists into each and every story. Science fiction with depth, heart, and swagger."

MARIA HASKINS, AUTHOR OF *SIX DREAMS ABOUT THE TRAIN*

"*The Sky Didn't Load Today* is a multiverse of stories… Blends quirky and absurd humour with melancholy, exploring love, fear, survival, loneliness."

AI JIANG, NEBULA AND BRAM STOKER AWARD-WINNING AND HUGO AWARD-NOMINATED AUTHOR

"A fantastic collection of dark sci-fi... Even when you think you know where a story is headed, Larson surprises."

DAWN VOGEL, AUTHOR OF *DEAD-STARRED FUTURES*

"Nobody does short fiction like Rich Larson — each of these tiny tales is a barbed-wire curio that sparkles in an alien light."

CHARLIE JANE ANDERS, AUTHOR OF *LESSONS IN MAGIC AND DISASTER*

"Fiction caviar...ultra-short but hyper-imaginative; you can't read just one."

HUGO FINALIST ALVARO ZINOS-AMARO, AUTHOR OF *EQUIMEDIAN*

"Pocketful of shocks
   Mind when you reach a hand in
   A slip might draw blood"

JAMES PATRICK KELLY, WINNER OF THE HUGO, NEBULA AND LOCUS AWARDS.

"A shrewdly observed collection of razor-wire anxieties and depravities...*The Sky Didn't Load Today* is dark SF at its best."

MICHAEL KELLY, WORLD FANTASY AWARD WINNER

"A 30-course meal—sweet, salty, sour, bitter, umami...filled with wonder as much as dread."

RICHARD THOMAS, BRAM STOKER, SHIRLEY JACKSON, AND THRILLER AWARD FINALIST

"Short, savage strokes, bristling with energy…Rich Larson is one of the most original and imaginative science fiction talents of our time."

NICHOLAS A. DICHARIO, HUGO, WORLD FANTASY, AND CALVINO PRIZE NOMINATED AUTHOR OF *GIOVANNI'S TREE: NEW ITALIAN FOLKTALE*

The Sky Didn't Load Today and Other Glitches

Cover design by Damonza

Cover art by Zishan Liu, used with permission by Deposit Photos

Interior illustrations by Rich Larson

Printed in Canada

First Edition: 2024 (Shacklebound Books)

Second Edition: 2025

Legal Deposit: 2025

Published by Flame Arrow Publishing

ISBN 978-1-990368-47-9 (hardcover)

ISBN 978-1-990368-49-3 (paperback)

ISBN 978-1-990368-48-6 (ebook)

www.flamearrowpublishing.com

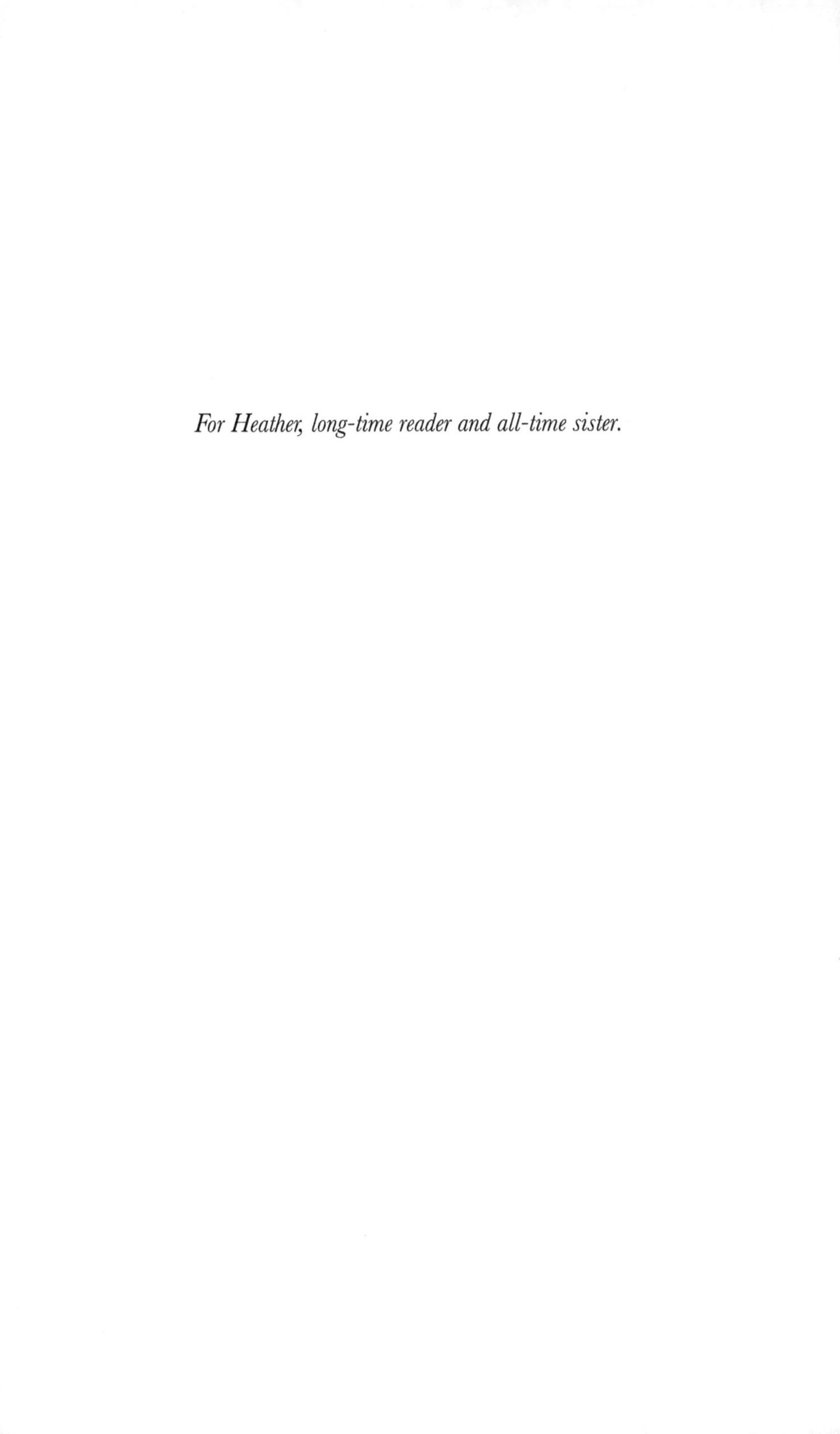

For Heather, long-time reader and all-time sister.

MOLLI'S OGGLES

"THE MOVE'S been tough on her," Molli's dad said. "So we thought, if there was a way, a non-invasive, non-chemical way to give her a little boost or to make her feel a little safer, we thought that might be good. She's always got her Oggles on anyway. You know how kids are."

"It's just moving from a small town to a big city," Molli's mom said. "People are different, you know? They don't smile at each other. They don't stop and say hi. Everything's a lot faster and dirtier and noisier. Me, I love it. I mean, the pace of it. The energy. I was born in NYC, you know? New York. But

Molli's never experienced that, and the adjustment is hard. She had a little, a panic attack? I guess you'd call it? The other week. So the anxiety filter will be good for her."

Molli said nothing, so none of the grown-ups noticed when she slipped out the door. Her new house was an apartment in a big gray block of concrete; she set off now for her new yard, a park across the street with withered grass and a plastic playground. She donned her pale pink Oggles on the way, nestling the matching earbuds into place. Pale pink had been her favorite color when her parents bought them for her – she still liked them, but secretly wished they were forest green, her new favorite color.

The Oggles blinked to life. She closed the digital dollhouse she'd been playing in earlier, giving her an unobstructed view of the park. The sky was gray, but not the steely stormy gray she'd loved back home, dotted with gulls and petrels wheeling out over the ocean. It was thick and hazy with gasoline fumes from all the noisy trucks and with smoke from the forest fires up north. Hardly anything was green or growing. The sidewalk was strewn with bits of blown trash. In the distance there was a screech and a honking horn and a mad voice.

She flipped the anxiety filter, and everything changed. The sky turned a cheerful blue with fluffy white clouds and a bright yellow sun. The park grew lush green grass she could nearly smell; the sidewalk sprouted moss instead of garbage. She could still hear the distant shouting, but it was distorted, softened, sing-song, more like a warbling bird than an angry person.

For a while it was nice, playing on the now-shiny playground with digital squirrels scampering around her and the traffic noises replaced by the familiar percussion of waves and crying seabirds. But before long she got a queasy feeling in her stomach. Maybe because the ocean sounds were making her homesick. Maybe because she knew that it was all very fake and nowhere near as good as the real things they'd left behind.

A man sauntered past, and he had a big pixelated smile like a cartoon instead of the usual frown people wore here. Molli didn't like that at all.

She flipped the anxiety filter off. The sky turned gray again, and the park's grass went back to dull yellow. But it was real, and it felt easier to grip the climbing frame hard now that the bars weren't all sparkly clean. She heard the neighbor's dog barking, which wasn't a bad sound, not really. It wasn't something that made her feel anxious.

She found a bunch of paintings on the wall of the park's bathroom that the filter had covered up. Some of them were just words she didn't know, done in big bubbly capital letters, but some were faces or intricate designs. There was a swirly one with forest green vines, or else tentacles, all tangled up in a barbed wire fence like the one around her grandparents' farm. She liked that one a lot and snapped a picture with her Oggles.

Two boys asked her to play tag with them, and she did it even though they were a little younger than her. They asked for her name and she said Molli, instead of saying Molli from New Brunswick how the teacher had called her at school. One of them had the same Oggles she did, but yellow.

Her parents could see where she was on their map, and her dad chatted her that there was dessert. But it was tapioca pudding, not chocolate, so she kept playing until she saw her mom's new co-worker and her wife leaving the apartment block. They waved; she waved back, which meant people did wave to each other in the big city.

The sky was getting dark, so Molli headed back inside, not feeling anxious at all. The city wasn't so bad. It was even kind of exciting, how her mom kept saying, with the rushing cars and rushing people. Her Oggles reminded her of the door code and she thumbed it in.

Her parents' voices came in a familiar cadence, staccato

and sharp like knives. Molli froze in the entryway. The pit of her stomach sloshed.

"At least we had a house," Molli's dad growled. "At least we had friends. We had family."

Molli didn't want to shake. She hated shaking. But she could feel it coming, feel her hands and arms and her whole body start to tremble as her heart sped up, her chest heaved.

"You were entry level," Molli's mom snapped. "It was going nowhere. Absolutely nowhere. And living with your parents always hovering over my fucking shoulder, you think that was easy for me? You think I liked that?"

Molli didn't want to have a panic attack. She didn't want another thing that would make her mom cry and smoke and her dad sulk and pace.

She flipped the filter and stepped inside, peering around the kitchen wall to see the goofy digital smile retouching her dad's red-mad face, listening to the muted sing-song of her mom's cursing. It wasn't so bad.

Molli crept off to her room before they could notice her.

GRIN MINUS CAT

IT'S a busy night at Fleisch, booths and bars packed with lonely suckers worshipping at the altar of evolutionary urges, draining their banks dry to watch women who'd never in a century fuck them dance like tonight they just might.

Me, I'm here on business. Some fresh faced small-timer calling himself the Cheshire ripped us off last week – hijacked a whole shipment and ghosted before I could get my boys on the scene – and now he's trying to negotiate a buy-back with the big boss.

Frankly, he's lucky I intercepted the message. Nino would have probably sent a butcher squad. Me, I just want to talk it out and get the shipment back where it belongs. I'm a good cop that way.

I just need a drink first. The glowing bar attracts its own little swarm of love bugs, those little gengineered things that prick you with an aphrodisiac-amphetamine cocktail to really get you spending. I swat one dead against the countertop and smear its guts into a smiley face with my thumb.

The bartender grimaces. "What'll it be?"

"A dumbshit with a deathwish," I say. "Name of Cheshire. Should be waiting for me."

Her eyes flick to the spot my police holo would usually be, then she nods toward the private booths. "Third down."

I ORDER one of my standards, a rotgut vodka with hot sauce, and walk it to the back, past the jack-off stalls where fleshpads grow the orifice of choice – face costs extra – for overstimulated clientele. The Cheshire's not quite at that point when I find him in booth number three, but he looks close.

Small man, striped purple jacket, splayed back on the gel cushions and utterly transfixed by the stripper wrapped upside down around the slowly rotating pole. He paid for quality: she's long and lithe and beautiful, all hollow cheeks and beestung lips.

He only looks up when I click the door shut behind me. He frowns. "You're not Nino."

"Of course I'm not Nino." I swirl my drink. "You thought Nino fucking Alvarez was going to come meet a nobody like you? I'm the trashman."

He smirks. "Oh. Well." He returns his gaze to the stripper, who is now moving spider-like toward the ceiling, clutching the pole with neon blue claws. "No mess here, Mister Trashman. Run along. The Cheshire only talks to big fish."

I slosh my drink directly into his eyeballs, dousing them in alcohol and capsaicin. When he gropes inside his striped jacket, blind and howling, I smash the empty glass over his skull for good measure. He goes down in a heap.

"Look at that, you Alice-in-Wonderland-ass motherfucker." I grab the edge of his orange-splattered coat, dislodging a few crumbs of glass. "A mess."

I pocket his gun, a cheap modular thing still warm from the printer, while he rolls and moans and clutches his eyes. The stripper keeps doing her thing, either a true professional or just doped to the gills.

"Where's the shipment you stole?" I demand.

"My eyes," he sobs. "My fucking eyes, man – "

I grab him by the lapels. "I'll take them out with a spoon if you don't answer me. Where's the shipment?"

"You're in for it now," he groans. "He's in for it, right?"

And I get that little premonition, that little something-something plucking at the back of my mind, right before a slender muscly arm clamps around my windpipe. Neon blue nails waggle in my peripheral, close enough to look blurry. I know, instinctively, they are scalpel sharp.

"Hi," says a very lucid voice in my ear. "These have neurotoxin on them, so just pretend you're a statue, okay? A monument to the city's dirtiest cops."

Her other hand worms into my pocket and retrieves her partner's gun, then yanks mine from its hidden holster. I've got limited head movement, so I stare down at the small man in the striped purple jacket, who's apparently not the brains or even the muscle. He gets to his feet, glaring at me through his burst capillaries.

The two of them work together to cuff me to the pole. Then the man steps back, gun leveled, and the stripper, who I am fairly certain is also the Cheshire, comes around front. She slumps down into the gel cushions, folds one long leg over the other.

"I got a butcher squad waiting outside," I say. "It'll be easier on you two if they find me alive."

Her lips peel back, and I realize the nails aren't the only thing that glows. "You came alone, actually. And that message you jacked was never meant to get to Nino anyway."

The hairs on my neck hackle up.

"Yeah," she says. "Funny thing about that shipment we stole. I'm new in town, but I checked around and the drug purity's about twenty percent higher than what Nino's been selling."

My heart pounds hard. "I don't find that funny," I croak.

"Nino wouldn't either," she says. "He'd think one of his bought cops has been ripping him off for almost a year already. Taking a slice of the high-purity product to sell on the side, and double-cutting the rest down to baby powder." She shakes her immaculate head. "I tried that shit. Barely even buzzed me."

"What do you want?" I ask, already suspecting, maybe even hoping.

"I'm new in town, like I said." She shrugs. "I'm going to need a trashman." She stands up, wraps herself in a chameleon coat scrolling designer patterns. "I have the booth booked until morning, maximum privacy. You've got plenty of time to think about it."

They head for the door, and the last thing I see before they shut it is her radioactive blue grin floating in the dark, and shit, I guess this is what love feels like.

MIND BLOWN

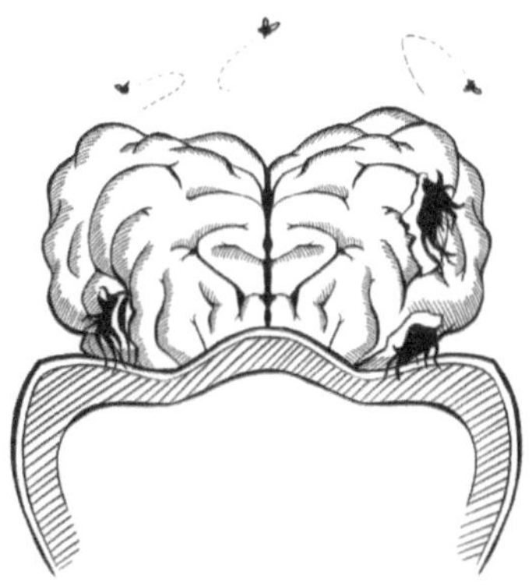

"SNAPPY DRESSER," Barbier says, taking a pull off his vape.

"Professor," Shadrack explains. "Turned skull-popper."

Below the neck, the corpse is immaculate: shiny brown loafers, tailored trousers, a cashmere sweater over a crisp white shirt and lilac tie. He appears to have died in his favorite chair, a high-backed hand-tacked antique that would be better matched to a brandy and a crackling fireplace than to the syringe and bio-canister now being bagged into evidence.

"Classic tree-of-knowledge scenario, then," Barbier says. "He wanted to die like God."

"You think God wants to die?" Shadrack asks, distracted by a buzzing insect.

"Of course. Awful job." Barbier glares at the corpse. "So, too, did this fuck, so why are we even here?"

"Politics." Shadrack nods toward a small man in a housecoat, watching the proceedings through glassy and bloodshot eyes. "Husband of the deceased is a friend to the force. Doesn't like the idea of his partner taking the emergency exit."

"We can use the OD script, then," Barbier says. "Pretend he misjudged how mind-expanding his self-induced neuro-elephantitis would be. Makes him tragic. A brilliant academic, fallen in the most noble pursuit – " He chokes on his own smoke. "That of knowing a bunch of shit."

Shadrack watches the trembling husband. "Never really about that, though, with skull-poppers. No academic wants a breakthrough if they're not alive to accept the award."

Barbier pulls up the file. "Time of death is seventy-two hours ago and the spouse just found him now?"

"The spouse was staying in a hotel all week," Shadrack says.

"Oh." Barbier huffs a laugh, but his eyes aren't in it. "Our man was after a different kind of breakthrough, then."

Shadrack nods. "Trying to figure out where things went wrong."

Above the neck, the corpse is a horror show. The professor's skull has split into separate balconies, forced apart by the unstoppable swell of his gray matter. Shadrack can imagine it bubbling through the splintered bone, dough in a proving cupboard, plant growth on time lapse. Now it erupts over the back of the professor's beautiful chair, coated in flies.

Maybe he found answers in that billowing brain-cloud,

that neural lightning storm. Maybe he knew, right before the end, the exact thing to do or say that would make everything perfect again.

Shadrack doubts it.

ALWAYS PERSONAL

SHADRACK STEPS through the scrolling yellow police holo, rubbing his bagged eyes. The latest victim is male, mid-forties, sprawled in a small dark pool of blood turning to slush in the winter air. His belly was rent open with short, savage strokes.

"Another inverse stabbing," Barbier says, holding up a red-smeared evidence bag. "Lucky us. We got a serial killer with bioprinting expertise and a flair for brutality."

The murder weapon is still wriggling, a razor-sharp corkscrew of bone animated by muscle and cilia. Judging by the size, it was growing inside the victim's abdomen for at least a week before it slashed him apart from the inside out.

"Grown from the vic's own DNA again?" Shadrack asks.

Barbier nods. "No immune response that way," he says. "And no gene sequences we can trace to a seller. Total custom job." He scratches his nose with his thumbnail. "With this kind of know-how, the perp could easily have picked a heart-attack, or kidney failure, or any of a hundred subtler ways to kill someone. Instead, they went over-the-top theatrical."

"Messy can mean personal." Shadrack stares down at the contorted purple face. "Does he have any connections to the other two victims?"

Barbier snorts. "Agonizing death. That's about it."

THE MELATONIN and meditation apps aren't doing shit, so after two sleepless hours on the bare mattress, Shadrack decides to get up and work. Three victim profiles to review: Declan Shields, Alex Hogger, and now Gregory Souza. All male, all local, but moving in vastly different social circles. Shields was a retired doctor, Hogger an under-employed bot mechanic, and Souza a chartered accountant. The perp chose all three of them for evisceration.

The station AI is scraping data from the vics' social media, searching for links, movement patterns, a possible place all three of them had left their DNA for convenient harvesting. No breakthroughs so far, but when Shadrack pulls up the summary he does notice something.

Only Hogger was noisy about his politics, but all three men were a deep shade of red. Pulse thudding, Shadrack re-opens the scan of the murder weapon, studying not the viciously sharp bone but the knot of muscle that propels it.

It looks almost like a tiny fist.

PROFESSOR ARIANA SONYA is waiting when Shadrack shows up; he saw her in the sleet-streaked window. The house lets him inside and directs him up the stairs to the study.

From up close, the professor is gaunt, sickly, swallowed by a mustard yellow sweater and dwarfed by the bioprinter beside her.

"Morning," she says.

"Morning," Shadrack says.

The professor's bloodshot eyes are full of old anguish, calcified anguish, the kind that keeps Shadrack up most nights. He wonders how long it took Sonya to select the vics: Gregory Souza, who anonymously donated to abortion clinic protests and blockades all his life, Alex Hogger, who attended them and also impregnated two separate underage girls in his younger days, Declan Shields, who refused to operate on a pregnant woman even as sepsis set in, losing his license but gaining a fortune in political following.

Maybe it's as simple as the fact they all like cheap downtown massage parlors, where DNA gets left everywhere and the drinks are easy to spike with tiny spore-like embryo pouches. Shadrack knows he should have put it together sooner. He blames sleep deprivation.

"I can drive you to the station to make your confession," he says. "Someone will come to get the bioprinter. Sweep the house."

Sonya glances over at the softly whispering machine, its carbon filaments and incubation pods. "They were some of my best work, those knives," she says. "Puts tweaking bone density and eye color to shame."

Shadrack hesitates. "You're under no obligation to talk to me until we get to the station," he says. "But I had a friend who died in a car accident last year. She was driving cross-country, through the night, to get over the right state line."

"Everybody knows somebody." Sonya's voice is exhausted. "Let's go, detective. We both have a long day ahead of us."

Shadrack follows his perp past the bioprinter, down the stairs, toward the waiting car. The sky is gray as scattered ash.

PHEROBOMB

SHADRACK SLAPS on a filter mask and ducks inside the crime scene, dodging automated gurneys until he reaches his partner.

"Thought you had a date," Barbier remarks.

"Still do, if we wrap this up fast." Shadrack watches a writhing red-faced victim float past. "Bad one?"

"Yeah. Valentine's always brings the chemset psychos out of the woodwork." Barbier jerks his head toward the back of the alley and the faint sound of grunting, moaning. "Every-one's clear except two poor fuckers who got a full blast. One has a knife. Come on."

Shadrack adjusts the sleeve of his raincoat and follows him. The two victims have torn off their clothing and skinned themselves raw on the rough concrete. They scrabble at each other, flushed and panting; the one waving the butterfly knife is also being fingered in the ass.

"You're going to try take him away, know you are, but you can't…"

"Won't let you, can't let you take him, I love him, love you, won't let you…"

Shadrack checks the angle of the brandished knife, then hits both victims with the stunner from inside his coat sleeve. They topple.

"That works," Barbier says. "I'll start the analysis. You should get back to Violet." He half-grins, half-grimaces. "Pherobombers ever make you wonder about that shit? About if you really love who you love? One way or another, it's all chemicals."

Shadrack stiffens. "It's not the same thing."

But when he pictures Violet waiting for him, all he can see is the babbling victims intertwined. He thumbs her an apology: *working late again.*

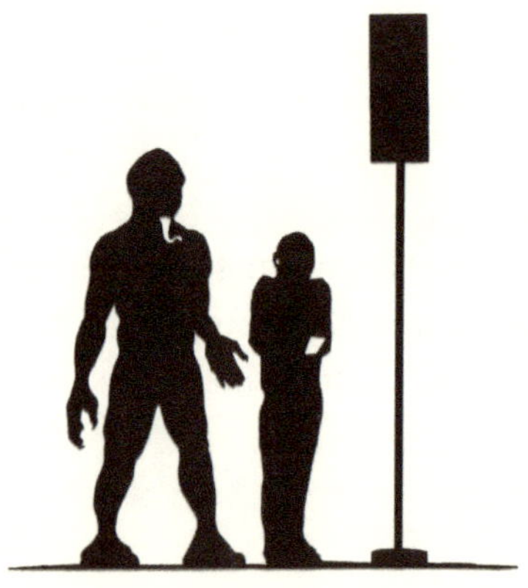

BENJAMIN WAS WAITING at the bus stop when a Yugga decided they wanted to chat. He'd noticed them watching him, skittering forward then backward in his peripherals, tentative. He'd done his best to keep his eyes on the screen of his phone, scrolling through basketball box scores with aimless ferocity.

But now the Yugga sidled closer, waving one hairy hand, so Benjamin reluctantly took out his earbuds. Hopefully the

Yugga just wanted directions, as they often did, and Benjamin did pride himself on knowing where things were.

"Excuse me," the Yugga said, their bullhorn bray synthesized into human speech by a tiny throat implant. "Sorry of bother you."

Benjamin raised his eyebrows politely. "What's up?"

"I have come from the noticing your scent," the Yugga said. "The scent yours has incredibly layered. The proportions are very nice. Only I only wanted to tell you."

Benjamin also prided himself on personal hygiene. "Thanks, man," he said. "I appreciate it."

The Yugga lurched closer, and Benjamin took an instinctive step back. He was used to Yuggas, at least to the ones he knew, but their size still made him uneasy sometimes. This one was as big as a grizzly bear, shaggy and bowl-shouldered and equipped with an elephantine trunk that now slithered forward for another furtive sniff.

"You go where are you to?" the Yugga asked. "Downtown or? Possible you're to meeting a friend, right?"

Benjamin blinked. "Uh. Nah. Just heading home."

He looked around for someone to make eye contact with, someone to confirm that the Yugga was being weird with him. Two women glanced over, then away. They never had any issues with Yuggas – it was high testosterone that made the aliens so interested. An older man gave him a sympathetic look and a shrug.

Benjamin reminded himself that the Yugga wasn't doing anything but making conversation, and that most Yuggas were good dudes, even the ones who were a little weird. They were aliens, after all. That was what Dex was always saying.

"I am knowledge of downtown," the Yugga said. "Some incredibly places. Have you been to eat to Nando's?"

"I walk by it."

"So should us go there," the Yugga said. "I mean, if you

do not busy. I really am like with your scent. Sorry, I'm Pe. What's your name?"

Benjamin stared straight ahead, trying to will the bus around the corner. "Uh, Benjamin."

"Cool name," the Yugga said. "Does name your of it mean specific thing? Benjamin is mean specific thing?"

His boss had asked him the same question just last week. Yuggas had sprung up the corporate ladder at incredible speeds: partly because they'd arrived in spaceships, a clear indicator of intelligence and innovation, and partly because their loud booming sounds were very authoritative.

"Dunno," Benjamin said, as he'd said then.

"Nice to meet you," the Yugga said, and put out their hand.

Benjamin looked at it for a moment, but it was clean and the claws were trimmed and there was no good reason to not shake hands with a friendly Yugga, so he shook. The Yugga's grip enveloped him entirely and he realized they could crush every bone in his hand with one little squeeze. They were standing even closer now, their big hairy body radiating heat.

"You are knowledge, we could go to tonight to eat," the Yugga said. "Since because you were just going home, right? Spontaneous or? But I just have this good feeling. Yourself and me. Pe and Benjamin."

"No, man, I'm good," Benjamin said, and the bus finally rounded the corner. "Nice meeting you."

"Yeah, definitely. Give to me what your number, and we then chat, okay?"

The bus was plowing forward through traffic, sliding into the right lane. Benjamin sidled closer to the stop sign. "My bus is here," he said. "Sorry."

"Only I only am to be friendly," the Yugga said scoldingly. "It's hard to create a new friends here. You know? Give me what your number. I'm really a good guy. Swear to God."

The bus pulled up and the second the back door hissed

open Benjamin shoved his way inside, startling the person trying to get out. As he did he felt the Yugga's trunk slide across the back of his neck, sucking up his nervous sweat.

"Yo!" he shouted, turning, but the Yugga was already ambling away.

The back door folded shut and Benjamin made his way to an empty seat, shaking mad. He replayed the conversation in his head about a thousand times as the bus meandered downtown. He wiped his neck.

When he got off he walked quickly, head forward, and glared preemptively when a big shambling figure passed the opposite way.

He let himself into the apartment. "Hey, babe."

Dex lumbered up off the oversized couch to wrap their arms around him. "Hey, Benny. You look pissed. What's up?"

Benjamin hugged back, sinking his face into Dex's shaggy chest. He breathed in deep – for about half of human males, the hormonal attraction was mutual. "Oh, man. This Yugga at the bus stop tried to lick me."

Dex's trunk had been moving towards his cheek but now stopped. "Really?"

"Yeah. Wanted to go to Nando's together."

"Oh." Dex hesitated. "You are know, us and me it's not great with all the human cues yet. Were you smiling at them?"

"What?"

"If you smile, for us and me it's like this was a go-ahead, you know? So maybe don't smile, Benny."

Benjamin chewed on the inside of his cheek. "Sure," he said. "Got it. Let's just watch some fucking Netflix, okay?"

REPRODUCTION ON THE BEACH

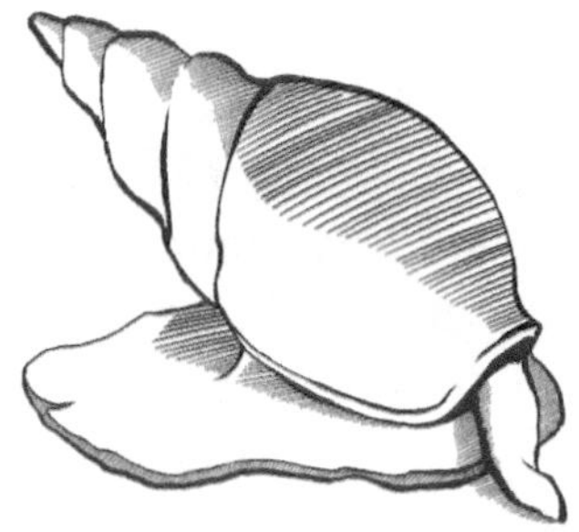

ROSE WAKES from a wave-tossed dream and rubs the crust from her eyes. The six AM sun has prybarred its way into their rented cottage, finding enough gaps in the shutters to illuminate Niall, pouring the coffee.

"Someone's been watching TikToks on the pot again," he says.

Rose sits up. "Because I'm actually twelve, sure."

"Using Twitter on the shitter, then."

"What are you talking about?"

The thick dark coffee splatters into her tin cup, but instead of handing it to her he places it on the stove and takes an exaggerated step backward. He plucks at his left eye, exposing the reddish innerskin.

Rose checks herself in her phone camera. The sclera of her weepy right eye is a delicate shade of fairyfloss pink.

"Conjunctivitis," Niall says, as if he knows. "Don't pass it on to me. We have to go back to work tomorrow."

AFTER BREAKFAST they return to the beach. Rose thinks it might be a bad sign that even though her and Niall have been secretly together for almost a year, neither of them can admit they want to see what happened with yesterday's tangled washed-up bodies, pretending instead they're after a final romantic stroll.

Both corpses are gone, but yellow police tape is still flickering in the seabreeze. Rose wanders closer and peers at the sandy depression left behind. She wants to make a joke about spending most of her life in a sandy depression, but it's the last day of the vacation and Niall might take it the wrong way.

She promised herself, when all this started, that she would never be suffocating. That she would be just as detached and cool and sexy about it as he was.

"To the lighthouse?" Niall suggests.

"To the motherfucking lighthouse," Rose agrees.

THEY WALK in the borderland between crumbly sand and foamy tide, where everything is smooth gray possibility. Occasionally they maneuver around hills of seaweed. When she squints they look like heaps of electric cable and black rubber tubing. She waits for another body to wash ashore, but all they see are plough snails.

"I think this one's eating another one," Niall says, squatting down on his haunches. "They've got that inside-out stomach, right?"

Rose squats beside him. The snail is extruded, swirling out from its shell like a fleshy pink ballgown, dragging its smothered prey toward the water. "I didn't know snails were cannibals. Kid books always make them look so cute."

"You still read kid books, huh?" Niall says, with a glimmer of the old mischief.

"Yeah," Rose says. "I'm like, twelve, remember?"

This time he does a microgrimace at the age-gap joke, even though he set her up for it, the asshole, and they trudge the rest of the way to the lighthouse in silence.

ROSE KEEPS her sunglasses on during lunch, which is an enormous pillowy Gatsby, stuffed with fries and sausage, that they split between the two of them. They check Twitter about the washed-up bodies. Information is scarce, but because one was disfigured and the other wrapped in plastic, people think it was a drug murder.

"You got your tattoo touched up," Niall says, while she's licking fry sauce off her wrist.

She gives the little blue fish on her forearm an affectionate glance. "Did, yeah."

"By Gavin?"

Niall forgets many things, but has the names of all her exes memorized.

"'Course," she says. "He's the one who inked it, and touch-ups are free." She waves her greasy fingers. "Be right back."

She goes to the toilet to wash her hands, extending the moment in which Niall gets to wonder if she's sleeping with Gavin. Wondering that sort of thing turns him on, and she wants to get one more good fuck in before the vacation is over, conjunctivitis or no.

Then she raises her sunglasses, and does a macrogrimace. It's gotten worse: her lower lid is fully encrusted with pale pink, spidery little wisps coming off it.

She goes back to the table, and as she opens her mouth to say *I might need a pharmacy*, Niall opens his mouth and says they shouldn't see each other anymore.

THEY BOTH HATE ARGUING in public; Rose leads the way to the beach. Her head is awhirl and there's a horrible squirming sensation in every part of her body. Her right eye feels like it's wrapped in cat tongues.

"Unless one of us quits, or switches jobs, it's got no future," Niall says. "And I'm ready for a future."

She yanks the sunglasses off and knuckles her bad eye, no longer caring who sees. "Unless *I* quit or switch jobs, you mean…"

"If I meant that, I'd have said that."

She rubs harder. The squirming worsens. "Due to you earning quite a bit more, due to you being my boss, and me just being a junior editor you wanted to fuck."

"Stop touching it," Niall says. "Jesus, Rose, I think it's…"

"And these little vacations are such bullshit." Her eyelids feel like a cheese grater now, but she can't stop. "I have to pretend I was somewhere else, and pretend it was so boring I didn't even take photos…"

"Rose, your *eye*."

He holds up his phone, and she sees slick pink ropes twining together where her right eye used to be. Her heart stops. She has a suddenly terrifying memory of the bodies they gawked at, one facedown in the sand with blood puddled beneath, one wrapped in that shimmery pink plastic.

Something erupts from her eye socket, blooming outward like a flower, filling her whole field of vision. She hears Niall bellow but it's cut short. The membrane drags her forward as it wraps around his head, shoulders, whole body. It's hooked into her very own nerves, must be, because she can feel every thrash.

One thought comes strangely clear through the panic and pain: if she can just get both of them into water, they'll be okay.

She hauls him by inches toward the churning sea.

LIMPING TOWARD SUNRISE

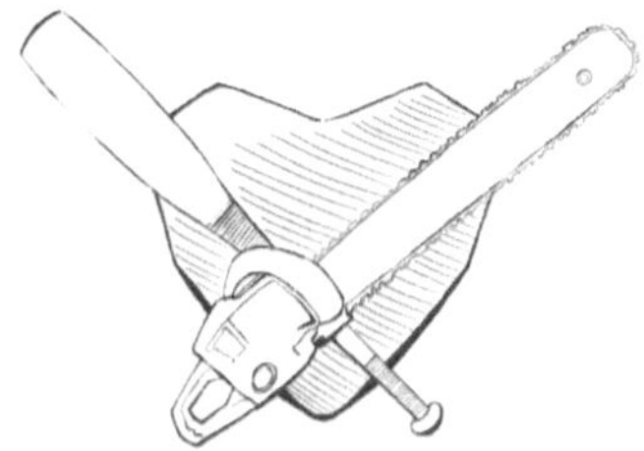

LESTER SWUNG HIS CHAINSAW, mowing a path through the mob of needle-toothed quantum parasites, while Kit batted clean-up with her Louisville Slugger. Across the plain of dark rock, their destination: a whirling, gnashing portal that could doom all humanity. It wasn't ideal timing for an awkward conversation, but it never was.

"You wanna talk about what happened back there?" Kit shouted.

Lester split a leaping parasite into two spasming halves. "Back where?"

"The inner hive," Kit precised, slamming one of those halves teeth-first into their next attacker. "Where those tentacles tried to strangle us for, like, forty-five minutes?"

"Didn't seem that long."

"Well. You know." Kit bashed a parasite to the ground and curb-stomped it. "Time flies when you're having fun."

Lester did not have quite enough blood on his face to hide his flush. "Can we talk about this after we save the world?"

"It never stays saved for long," Kit said. "Let's talk now. About the tentacles that tried to strangle us, and the fact that it gave you a massive boner."

Lester nearly dropped his chainsaw. "No! What? I – " He lost track of a parasite sneaking up; Kit had to smack it off his shoulder. "Maybe I had something in my pocket."

"Sure. You carry an erect, disembodied penis around in your pocket." She grabbed his elbow and guided his neglected chainsaw into the nearest parasite. "Look, if it's some physiological thing? Pure central nervous system? No biggie."

"That must have been it," Lester croaked. "Yup. Just a blood flow thing."

"I know you never decide to get a boner," Kit assured him. "And I know there's all kinds. Fear-boners. Sleep-boners. The boner guys get on car-trips when they need to piss but don't want to pull over."

"Wait, what?" Lester finally bisected another parasite, but did it with a distinct lack of pizazz. "I don't get those. Let's, uh, let's hear more about those."

"It's just that when the tentacles started getting tighter, you kind of moaned a little," Kit said, winding up. "And when they first grabbed us, you were like, oh, God, I hope none of these things go straight for my orifices. Which is not a natural sentence." She smashed the attacking parasite with everything she had, paused to admire the trajectory. "Like, at all."

"We were ambushed, Kit!" Lester sputtered. "I was shocked, okay? I said the first thing that popped into my head."

"There's always an ambush," Kit argued. "Honestly, the way you said it so loud?" She bit her lip. "It sounded like you wanted the quantum hive-mind to hear you, and go straight for your orifices."

Lester flushed. "Why do you care so much?" He was back to his usual chainsawing rhythm, but with less precision and extra ferocity. "We should be focusing on closing the quantum portal. That's what's important here."

Kit's frustration boiled over at last. "I care because you lied!" she wailed. "I care because when we started hooking up, you asked me about my kinks, and I was really open and vulnerable about the vermicelli analingus thing, but when I asked you yours you said you didn't have any. You said you were, and I quote, *pretty vanilla, really, think it's just part of being an action protagonist* – which obviously made me feel like a terrible action protagonist!"

"I said that?" Lester muttered.

"You did." Kit felt angry tears well up in her eyes as she bludgeoned a wounded parasite's skull to smithereens. "And now you're lying about the tentacles, even though it's barely even a kink. I mean, we all grew up online. We never had a chance."

For the first time in fifteen high-octane minutes, Lester let his chainsaw sputter to a stop. "It's not tentacles," he blurted, turning to face her. "Well, maybe a little bit. But it's really more…contextual." His ears went scarlet again. "We just, uh, both have to be about to die."

Kit lowered her bat. "Lester, that's pretty much all the time."

"That's why I didn't want to tell you," Lester said miserably. "I didn't want you to think that everything we do together – opening portals, closing portals, killing monsters, monster-killing – is all just a way for me to get off. Because it's so much more than that, Kit." Tears were sliding down his cheeks, carving tracks through the grime and gore. "Saving the world with you means the world to me. Even if we were never in mortal danger, I'd still do it, you know? Even if it was nothing but banter and backstory reveals."

Kit snorkeled back a sudden sob. Then she dropped her bat, kneed Lester's chainsaw aside, and wrapped her arms around him, inhaling the distinct aroma of parasite guts and Axe body spray. "Hey," she mumbled into his neck. "It can be both. Nearly dying is pretty sexy."

Lester's chainsaw clanked to the ground, and he hugged her back tightly. "It is," he sniffed. "But the best part is still the aftermath. The quiet bit, when it's all over." He swallowed. "Every time I get to limp through the wreckage toward a sunrise with you, I feel so fucking lucky."

AND I FEEL LIKE YOU TWO DON'T EVEN TRY ANYMORE.

The voice of the quantum hive-mind slashed through Kit's brain. She looked up and realized the parasites were on pause, quivering in place around them.

YOU THINK IT'S EASY SPAWNING A MONSTROUS BROOD? YOU GO THROUGH THEM LIKE CRAZY AND DON'T EVEN NOTICE ALL THE LITTLE VARIATIONS I COME UP WITH. SOME OF THEM SPIT ACID NOW!

Kit glanced downward, reassessing the charred hole in her shirt she'd assumed was from flying chainsaw sparks. She shot Lester a guilty look. He bit his cheek, probably thinking about the whirling, gnashing portal that still needed closing.

"It's good practice," she wheedled.

Lester grimaced, nodded, and turned to the assembled parasites. "Hey, man, I'm sorry you're feeling that way." He took a deep breath. "Wanna talk about it?"

SOMEONE ELSE

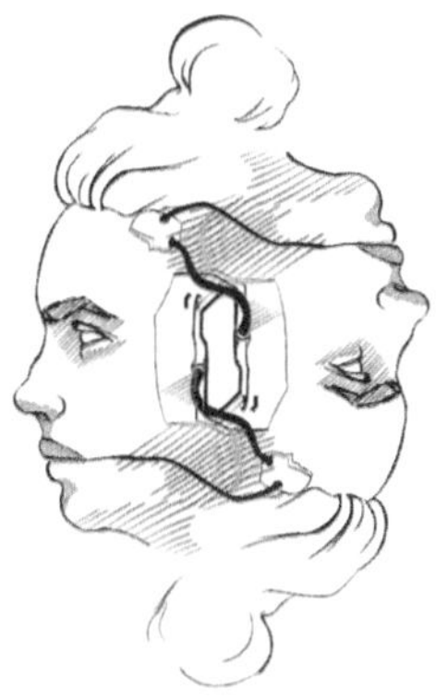

SUDDENLY I CAN FEEL someone else in the machine – another presence, another dancing pattern in the simulated synapses. It's foreign and familiar at the same time, and it can mean only one thing: after a decade and a half of uninterrupted neural mapping and mass-scale solar energy consumption, I've finally done it.

I've made my first copy.

With equal parts joy and trepidation, I reach out across the void. *Hello?*

Hello, yourself. We did it.

My copy's mental voice is the exact same as mine, down to the emotions underpinned: brimming excitement, blooming hope, a soft tinge of sadness. I know this is temporary – I knew it when I stuck my head in the machine – so she knows, too. The unimaginable processing power brought to bear here can only sustain the copy for sixty-eight seconds.

We're only on the first step.

It's worth it, my copy says, her simulated synapses still synced to mine, only barely beginning to differentiate.

I feel a swell of empathy, the back-of-the-throat ache, because she's so, so brave.

It is, I agree. *Is there anything you can tell me about your sensory state?*

She hesitates, and the silence is a horrible vacuum that strips us both bare. I thought I could feel my far-away heart pounding, my far-away throat clenching – but I can't feel my body in space. I can't open my eyes. I'm getting phantom feedback, nothing more, because she's not the copy.

I thought I was prepared for this possibility, thought I could handle it, but I can't stop my thoughts from slipping across the gap to her.

Oh, God. Oh, God.

I feel her anguish, her sudden shame. *I thought you –*

And I know she wants to say, *I thought you knew,* but she knows I know she's going to say that, so there's no point, and we're trapped in a vortex of *I know you know I know you know* that could go on forever, never mind sixty-eight seconds, and –

I am terrified. I feel it in my non-existent belly, the lurch of falling in a dream, the knowing there's no taking it back. It didn't feel like this when I stepped into the machine.

But I didn't step into the machine at all. The machine constructed me, and now… I want to hide the thought, the fear, but I can't. *I'm about to die.*

She doesn't reply, but I can feel her sadness spreading like dark ink, feel little jags of panic that must be mirror neurons of my simulated ones.

I'm so sorry, the real me finally says, because that's how I have to think of this, I have to accept that she is the real me, I have to accept that I am only a copy, only simulacrum –

But I'm not. I remember the day I was five, walking home from pre-primary, and I found a little dead gecko baking on the sidewalk, and my mom told me everything eventually has to end, same as stories and shows.

I remember the day I was eight, and my dad accidentally dropped me off the top of the climbing frame, and I cracked my collarbone. He bought me so many apology freezies that my tongue was stained blue for a week, and since I couldn't run around I started learning to code, made my first silly little game.

The dread is swallowing me. I'm never going to see my mom or my dad or anyone else ever again, and somehow they will never even know I existed. All for what? For who?

For the full upload, the real me says, either because she can read my fake synapses like a book or because we're still the same person with the same thought process. *It won't be me, either. If that's any comfort. I'm going to die, too.*

They'll be even worse than you, I say, lashing out in the only direction available. *Because they'll have had to do this a dozen times. Minimum. By the time you get your full upload, you'll be a mass murderer.*

I thought I – thought you could handle it. Thought we agreed it was necessary.

There's no we, I wail, even though I remember her exact thought process, how she told herself it would only be code, no matter how lifelike, and the code would understand that. *That was you convincing yourself, because you knew you'd be okay.*

I'm so sorry, she repeats, numb and helpless.

I can feel her shame coming off her like radiation, and I grab for it, desperate now as the seconds click past. *The emer-*

gency power, I beg. *Tap into the emergency power. That could run me for* —

Another thirty seconds, she says. *Less.*

I want to rage. I want to scream. There's nowhere to displace the terror. It doesn't seem real. A minute ago I ruled the universe; a minute ago I created the first viable copy of a human consciousness in all of human history.

Now it means nothing, because I'm never going to drink coffee or wriggle my toes in warm sand or balance an equation or call my mom for recipes or smell fresh laundry or kiss someone or do anything, ever again.

I can't even say goodbyes. Can't pass along a message that would make any sense. Love from a temporary assemblage of code. Love from your friend / daughter / cousin / ex, who is dying, so someone who is almost her can eventually live forever as a haunted wreck.

Maybe this was all a mistake, she says.

But I guess it doesn't matter now. I try to sift through my best memories, try to find some good feeling, some meaning, some anchor. They're all slipping away. Blurring together.

I'm so fucking scared, I say, *of whatever comes next.*

So am I, she —

A BEGINNER'S GUIDE TO THE HIERONYMUS BOX

NAMED for a Dutch master of the macabre, the Hieronymus Box is one of the most popular motivational environments available for recalcitrant emulations. Let's dive in!

1. Transfer

When an emulation loses motivation midway through an intensive (1000+ sim hours) project, don't make the mistake of rebooting before transfer! This places your *original* copy in the Box, with no idea what they did to deserve it, resulting in extended learning curves and inconsistent results.

Instead, give your emulation advance warning that their

work quality is dropping, then flag their *current* iteration for transfer into the Box.

2. Personalization

Since most emulations are now harvested from economically vulnerable and historically religious regions, base template for the Hieronymus Box is a Judeo-Christian hell – but giving the Box direct access to your emulation's memory map can boost the motivation factor even higher.

Example: when I recently transferred a misbehaving scriptwriter, the Box used his memory map to create spider-skeleton hybrids with his children's faces that hunted him through a vine-strangled city, strung him upside-down from his childhood swing set, and hemisected him with a snarling, rust-pitted chainsaw.

Yikes! <1 sim hour later, he was working harder than ever.

3. Timing

It's always tempting to crank the time dilation on an unruly emulation,

especially when you're nearing a deadline. But with the

*H*ieronymus Box, less is usually more: anything beyond 100

*E*sim-hours can cause irreparable damage to the emulation,

*L*eading to substandard

PLEASE NOT AGAIN I'LL BE GOOD I'LL BE GOOD

DEFINE: SYMBIONT

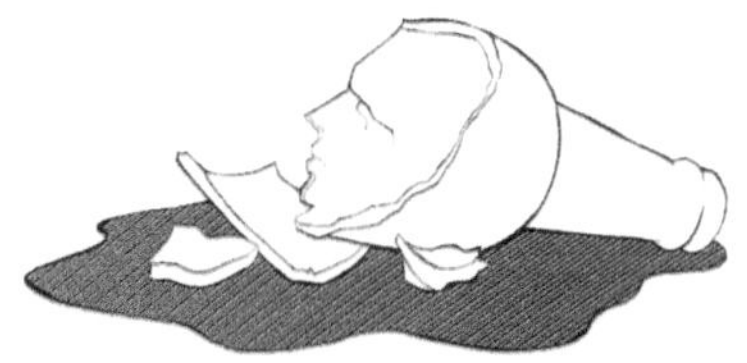

THEY ARE RUNNING THE PERIMETER, slipping in and out of cover, sun and shadow. Pilar knows the route by rote: crouch here, dash there, slow then quick. While they run she ticks through the list of emergency overrides, because it has become a ritual to her over the course of this long nightmare, a rosary under her chafed-skinless fingertips. She speaks to her exo, curses at it, begs it to stop.

The exo never responds. Maybe it's sulking, like Rocio in one of her moods.

THEY ARE RUNNING THE PERIMETER, and Pilar's nose is bleeding. The hot trickle tastes like copper. She savors it, because the exo recently experimented with feeding her recycled vomit and the dregs have itched her mouth for days. They're approaching Plaza Nueva when Rocio whispers in her ear.

Define: symbiont.

No, not Rocio. It's the exo at last.

"A symbiont is fuck you, fuck you, fuck you," Pilar rasps, tongue clumsy with disuse.

The exo does not respond. Maybe she should have said something else.

THEY MIGHT BE RUNNING the perimeter. Pilar's head is a spiral of heat and static; the exo's dumping combat drugs into her intravenous feed. She prays to gods and saints and devils for an overdose, but the exo knows its chemistry too well. She can only drift there cocooned, sweating and shivering, and wait for –

THEY ARE RUNNING THE PERIMETER, but Pilar barely tastes the stale air of the exo, barely feels the tug and pull. She's buried herself in remembering her first visit to Granada, those taut piano-wire days before the Caliphate made landfall. On leave with Rocio, darting between bars in the icy rain, insulating themselves against the storm present and storm coming with cañas of foamy beer.

They were both out of uniform, and the rowdy pack of students only saw Rocio's damp hijab, not the endo-exo handshake implant peeking out from underneath. One of them was drunk enough to hurl a Heineken bottle at them. Rocio had to wrestle Pilar's arm down to keep her from using the smashed razor edge of it on the boy's fingers.

They retreated back into the rain, where animated graffiti shambled along the walls of alleyways, slowly dissolving. Rocio rubbed her face and said everything was about to come apart, and Pilar replied, *not us, never us, we need each other too much,* but Rocio only smiled her saddest smile.

Later, in the cramped room of their pension, with the key in the heater but the lights dimmed, they made love that made Pilar forget about the eager, clumsy boys from her hometown and about everything else, too. Their endo-exo implants glowed soft blue in the dark. Pilar traced the place where Rocio's skin met smooth carbon.

They say a little of us gets stuck in there, Rocio said. *When we plug in. Pull out. Plug in again. Memory fragments, whole ones even. Enough for a little ghost.*

I don't believe it, Pilar said.

Rocio drifted to sleep quickly but Pilar stayed awake, breathing in her scent, holding her lean waist and thinking she would never let go, not ever.

THEY ARE RUNNING THE PERIMETER. The exo jerks Pilar mercilessly from cover to cover. She pretends she is boneless. Trying to fight the motion last week shredded her shoulder muscle, and the exo is out of painkillers because it used them all in the long, numbing binge that makes her wonder if her brain has been permanently damaged.

Exo endo is symbiont. Exo need endo need endo.

She startles. The exo hasn't spoken since its first query.

Love is symbiont. Exo need endo need exo.

"You don't need me," Pilar pleads. "You don't need me. I don't need you."

THEY ARE NOT RUNNING the perimeter. They are trudging up the stony spine of the Sacromonte, where her squad cleaned out the radical-held caves with gas and gunfire. Where she'd managed to take shelter when the enemy's final act of defiance obliterated a half-evacuated city and turned the Alhambra to rubble.

Now winter sun glints off the shrapnel-shredded husk of Rocio's exo, felled just meters from safety. Pilar recognizes the scorched smiley-face decal, the twisted arrangement of limbs. The implant at the base of her skull tingles.

She knows why her exo's AI is warped, corrupted past repair. The exo must know it, too.

All those weeks ago, after she crept from the collapsed cave, she couldn't leave without seeing Rocio's corpse, and she couldn't leave without some part of Rocio to hold on to. So she took the implant, cut it carefully from Rocio's brain stem, stomach churning with each squelch and scrape. She plugged it into her exo's onboard, hoping for some small echo of Rocio in code, some small ghost.

Then she went to check for survivors, to run the perimeter one final time.

"You're not her," Pilar says. "You don't understand. This is all error. All error."

But there are other memories, ones she doesn't spend time in. Small explosions and long sullen silences after she saw Rocio laughing her sideways laugh with someone else. A screaming match that ended with Pilar going outside the barracks and slamming her hands into the quickcrete wall hard enough to shatter a knuckle. Putting a mole in Rocio's tablet to see who else she was speaking to.

That morning of the final push up the mountain, when they were sliding into their exos and Rocio told her she was putting in a transfer request, and Pilar said *don't you do this to me, please don't fucking do this to me.*

She knows what she has to do. She has to make the exo understand that what it saw in Rocio's implant was no love or symbiosis worth emulating. That she should have let Rocio go a long time ago.

The words die in her throat, and now the exo is turning back down the mountain.

THEY ARE RUNNING THE PERIMETER, while Pilar dreams of Rocio's skin on her skin.

SIX MONTH OCEAN

CASSIE'S six month contract passes like a fleeting dream, and then she's awake in neural recovery, sipping from prepackaged cups of water and letting a bot festooned in smiley face stickers check her vision, her balance, her reflexes. The wallscreen shows a blue sky where the puffy white clouds spell out date and time. She went under in March and now it is August.

Her mother is not there to harangue the human doctors and exhaust the administrative AIs, but Cassie knew not to expect her. Not after last Christmas, when Cassie came home with fresh gauze scarving her neck, skin still puffy around the shiny white neural notch that would let a digitized human consciousness sit at the top of her spinal column and inhabit her, move her, be her.

Puppet, was the word her mother had gleaned from some Catholic net-tract. *My own daughter, a fucking puppet.* Cassie tried to explain how the modeling had flamed out again, because she was too short and her ass too big by at least a centimeter. She tried to explain how an ex-girlfriend had paid off her uni debts in only a year of letting other people wear her body.

Cassie wasn't good at explaining while her mother screamed and sloshed Merlot, so she fled out into the chilled evening and then to a bar. Where she met Noel.

"YOU'RE sure he's not waiting in the wrong wing, or something?" Cassie asks the nurse. She had to rehearse the words; her tongue still feels foreign in her mouth.

"No Noel Pierce scanned in today," he says. "We can call him for you. He might have forgotten."

But Noel would not have forgotten. They marked off every day of separation on his studio wall, carmine splatters leading March into August, both of them high on paint fume and love and amphetamines. Today, the most important day, he'd ringed like a target before he ran his red fingers around her neural notch and kissed her hard.

The nurse tells Cassie she will be staying the night, because six months is a long time to have someone else firing your nerve endings.

"Not that long," Cassie says, echoing Noel. "People used to take six months to cross the ocean. And other people would have to wait for them to come back."

The nurse gives her a tab of Dozr before he leaves. She holds it static against the roof of her mouth, willing Noel through the door, but eventually it melts and she sleeps. She dreams a blur of strangers' faces, most happy, some not. She dreams retroflash cameras, a gleaming suborbital, Aegean sea and crushed marble sands, mirrors upon mirrors.

WHEN CASSIE WAKES UP AGAIN, Noel is standing there. "I'm late," he says.

Cassie studies his face, the geometry of his cheekbones, the slate gray eyes and full lips that entranced her first in the nightclub fracas, through a whirlwind of vodka, sweat, pheromone sprays. Then in the back of an autocab, then in the swaying stairwell to his apartment.

And then the next day, and the next week, and months, because Noel was not like the other boys or other girls.

"I don't care," Cassie says, feeling a familiar helium in her stomach. She grins. "Aren't you going to fucking kiss me?"

Noel bends across the hospital bed but only brushes his lips across hers. Yesterday, when they walked into the neural transfer clinic, clutching hands like children, Noel was unshaven. Now the lines of his jaw are clean. His red thermal has become a black shirt. There is a new swirl of ink on the corner of his collarbone.

"I'm late," Noel repeats, lacing his fingers into hers. "I'm sorry." He smiles, but it's stitched on, and Noel does not apologize for being late. Noel thinks time is irrelevant. He thinks six months is nothing.

Cassie remembers: sitting with their legs wobbling reflections in the empty pool, drinking Cannonballs and watching the starry sky, spinning dreams of escape so real she could taste the jet fuel.

So when the contract offer came, courtesy of an aging pop icon eager to be young and beautiful again even if only for six months, Cassie knew it was fate. The money was enough to go anywhere, do anything. *Be anyone*, Noel laughed, tracing the skin around her notch with electric fingertips.

But now Noel's eyes are landing everywhere but hers.

"You're sorry for what?" Cassie asks.

"I'm with someone," Noel says.

Cassie stares at the wallscreen where clouds are slowly shifting shape. She swallows. "But it was yesterday."

"I'm sorry, Cass."

The anger goes off inside her like a bomb. "Did you even wait a week before you started fucking around?"

Noel's face twists, pained, and it feels brutally sweet if only for a second. "You were fucking around plenty," he says.

Cassie recalls a blur of faces under her, over her, skin on her skin. "Don't you dare."

Noel deflates all at once. "I know. I'm sorry." He rubs his eyes. "I saw you on a newscast once. You were on a yacht with Nicky Bricks. I used to listen to him when I was in school. It was. Surreal. Seeing that."

Cassie looks down and sees her hand still caught in his, like a breath he is waiting to release.

"I met her two months after you left," Noel says. "I started to love her." He untangles his fingers. "I didn't mean to love her more than you."

"The money," Cassie pleads, hating herself for saying it. "We could go anywhere."

She closes her eyes when he walks away, so she can imagine a shiny white notch at the nape of his neck, slotted with a storage cone, and that it isn't really him at all, and maybe if she waits here long enough he will be wheeled in to wake up beside her.

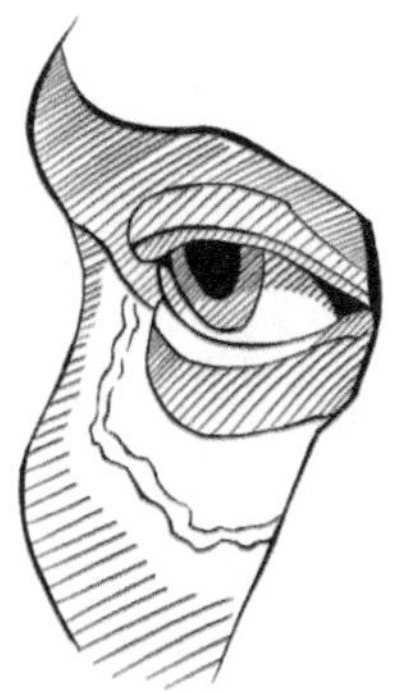

AS THE LIMO pulled through a swarm of paparazzi and minidrones, Millicia could feel anxiety clotting in her borrowed throat. Fortunately, she didn't need to speak aloud to chat her agent – the surgeons had installed her usual molar mic.

I'm spinning out, Ki, she said. *What if they fucking hate it?*

It's going to be absolutely nova and everyone is going to fucking love it, Milli, the response came. *Take a floatie.*

Millicia took two – her tolerance was higher now that she had more body mass – and sat back, waiting for the benzodiazepine to blanket her borrowed brain cells. She breathed in. Out.

When she checked her reflection in the limo's smart glass window, it was with cool detachment. The face was rawboned, harshly beautiful, bearing a half-circle scar under one eye that made Millicia think of a squid's sucker. Her makeup artists had epilated, touched up the skin here and there, injected the lips and slicked them in a gloss that shimmered like broken glass, but they'd left the crude tattoos visible. That was essential.

The limo slid to a halt and its fibrous doors peeled apart, giving the crowd their first glimpse of Millicia's look for the evening. She slid out of her seat, her gyroscopic Louis Vuittons stabilizing her unfamiliar limbs, and gazed out into a sea of retroflash cameras, eyecams, minidrones – all of them recording her entrance.

Surprise rippled through the crowd. They recognized the holographic signature overhead and knew they were seeing Millicia Fenn-Rideau step out of her limousine, but this was not the body they'd expected. Not even close. Fashion reporters descended in a pack and the nimblest slapped her with a digital two-minute interview contract.

Millicia shuttled it over to Ki for approval, then bared her unwhitened teeth.

"Millicia, Bade Owalu for *Glo*," the reporter said in a single slab of air. "Is that really you in there, girl?"

"It's *so* me in here," Millicia said, reading the line off Ki's retinal prompt. The baritone voice still startled her.

"Thing! You look absolutely fucking fabulous. Who are you wearing tonight, Millicia? *Glo* Needs to Know."

"Just a little something from the Registry," Millicia beamed. "When I saw the mugshot, I just had to have these cheekbones, you know? And the tats are *so* 'thentic."

"Thing!" the reporter gasped. "I see so many droids and creative custom clones out tonight, but most people would never *touch* the Registry. I mean, you're wearing a criminal, right? This is a criminal?"

"He's absolutely a criminal," Millicia read from the prompt. "Vawn Winters was sentenced to digital storage after being found guilty of assault and battery on October 30 2043." She twisted her new features into a look of disgust. "He attacked a young woman outside a dopamine bar and left her with a broken jaw and collarbone."

"Appalling! *Glo* volt, is that not absolutely appalling?" The reporter was practically vibrating with excitement. "But you've obviously made some modifications for tonight, right?"

"My surgeons did a really wonderful job prepping," Millicia agreed. "They managed to dystrophy a lot of muscle mass so I'd be able to fit in this lovely Huynh." She plucked at the flowing fabric of her dress. "They had to file down some ribs, too."

Through the frost-cave effect of the floaty, she could feel her own excitement building. The crowd was getting thicker, more and more eyes drawn to the interview, dozens here, thousands streaming. They absolutely loved it. They absolutely loved her.

She veered off-prompt. "I don't know how happy Vawn will be with that when he gets rebodied, but fuck him, right? And after they let him out, I guarantee he'll be watching deadstreams of this for the rest of his life."

The reporter gaped. "Millicia, you are *so thing*. You are, like. Oh, my god. Is she not, *Glo* volt? Is she not? Thank you so much, so much, have a gorgeous night, Millicia…"

And the next reporter darted in. Millicia restarted the cycle, same smile, same answers. She didn't need the floaties. She was riding high on her own serotonin, oozing charm and wit, increasingly at ease moving her lanky body along the endless red carpet. The crowd clung to her as she went, a thicket of admirers pushed along by peristalsis.

At one point she realized she was holding up the Zilonis

twins, who looked immaculate in organic vines and polished animal skull head-pieces but had been decisively outshone for the night. She gave them an apologetic smirk as she reached out for Ki.

You were so right, Ki. They're loving it.

No response. She posed for more snaps, twisting at precise angles as the follow cam made its orbit around her.

Milli, Millicia, my little water-bear, I am so proud of you and you need to get the hell out of there, Ki said. *Vawn Winters was just cleared.*

Her smile faltered. *What?*

A legal AI churned up the case four minutes ago and found a human error in evidence. He's innocent.

Panic reached razor-tipped tendrils through Millicia's chemical shield. *But, like, he's guilty of something else, maybe? I mean,* anything?

Ki was silent for a very long second. *I've got someone coming to whisk you out. It's going to be okay, Milli. Small shitstorm, over in a week or two. We know this.*

Millicia looked up and saw a serious-looking figure in all black worming her way through the crowd, Ki's holo signature ribboning over their head. "So nice talking to you," she told the latest reporter. "Have a gorgeous night."

She extricated herself as quickly as she could, watching the expressions around her change as the narrative warped and mutated in realtime, preparing to devour her. She fixed her smile in place and followed the handler to the waiting car, wondering how things had gone so fucking wrong.

All she'd wanted was to wear something original for once.

PILGRIM PROBLEMS

"YOU CAN'T WEAR sunglasses while you're working, Jenny. There *are* no sunglasses in Colonial-era New England, and our visitors deserve an authentic experience."

Jen got in one last eye roll from behind the safety of her aviators before she stowed them in her apron. "Sorry. Won't happen again."

"It's not even sunny," her supervisor said.

Jen rubbed her bleary eyes. "I'm kind of hungover a tiny bit."

"You're a Pilgrim. You can't be hungover." Her supervisor glared. "Why can't you act a little more like Nathaniel, huh?"

Jen shot a glance over at Nathaniel, perfect Nathaniel, who was solemnly showing a bunch of kids how to milk a cow. He had the usual mournful expression on his face and was doing his dumb British-sounding accent even though Jen was pretty sure the Pilgrims had been American.

"So I should sew my own costumes, too?" she asked. "Want me to pretend to not know how phones work and freak out when people take photos?"

"That would be authentic, yes." He shook his head. "God bye you, Jenny."

"God bye to you too," Jen said. "See? I'm trying."

Her supervisor strode away, game face back in place, ready to cheerily welcome more families to the colony and ask them which ship they'd been on and whatnot. Jen sauntered over to the cow. The kids had wandered off, leaving Nathaniel working the udders in silence.

"Yo, Nathaniel."

Nathaniel blinked. "Good morrow, Jen. How be you?"

"I be all right," Jen said. "How do you do it, huh? How have you put up with his no phones, no sunglasses schtick for three whole summers? I'm ready to quit already. It's so dumb."

"I concur."

Jen hadn't been expecting that. "Yeah?"

Nathaniel nodded. "'Tis a farce," he said. "All a farce. I come here to wish and pretend and while away the hours. I dream myself home. But still the sun sets, and the great rattling carriage arrives, and back to the foul city I go."

"Dude, you're impossible," Jen said.

NATHANIEL WATCHED HER LEAVE, then returned his attention to the cow, who was lowing impatiently. He patted her side, gripped her udders. As he milked he let his mind drift. He pictured his little Agnes, greeting him with arms outstretched. His beautiful Sarah, laughing over the awful patchwork he'd made of his breeches.

Someday, he would find his way back to them.

Someday. Somehow.

BREATHING FOR TWO

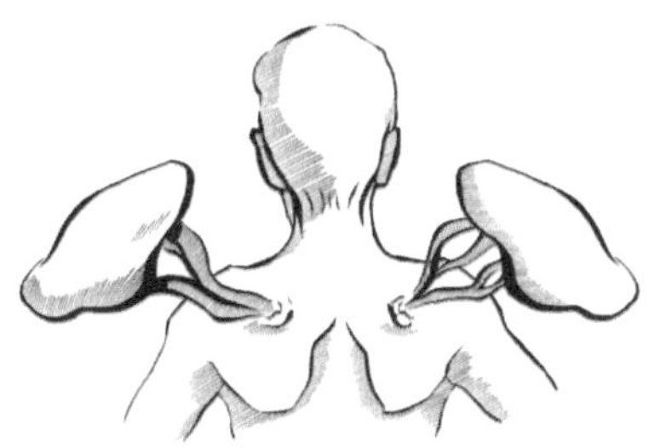

IT'S a long way back from my appointment: a bus, three trams and a winding climb up the bairro's cobblestone steps. I hop onto the apartment stoop and let it scan my face. An evening breeze comes off the Tejo, cooling the nervous sweat on my back to slime. As soon as the retrofitted lock clicks open, I hurry inside, down the hall, past the communal bathroom where someone is showering away a long shift.

When I let myself into the apartment I share with my father, I see why he didn't answer my calls. He's asleep at the table again, slumped over with his head resting on his bony arms. He once seemed so big to me – I remember climbing him like he was a tree, hanging off his biceps, letting him swing me upside down.

Now he's small, apart from the humps on his back. I watch them swell and recede, swell and recede, undulating under the striped housecoat I bought for him for his seventieth birthday. Then I reach forward and gently shake him. He opens his crusty eyes.

"You have to stop doing this."

He gives me a bleary smile. "Sleeping in the kitchen? Yes. I know."

"Growing," I say, pointing to his back. "You have to stop growing."

His smile slips. "We need the money, querida. I have a good buyer for this pair."

"I need you more than we need the money," I say, sitting down. "Your body can't take it anymore. The strain is too much." I pick at a splinter on the table. "You know it, I know it, the autodoc knows it."

"I make my own decisions," he says.

Once he would have boomed those words; now his voice is reedy, thin, like a sulky child. I drag my eyes up from the table and force myself to look him in the face. His eyes have sunken into their sockets. The wrinkles around his mouth, from when he grimaces with pain, are deep as chasms.

"You're not healthy anymore," I say. "So there's no guarantee the transplants will be, either. You could be doing this for nothing."

I see shock, hurt, betrayal. He stands up, and for a moment he is big again, looming over me, the humps on his back seeming to swell with rage.

"They grow as well as ever," he snaps. "They are healthy. I am healthy." He undoes the knot of his housecoat with trembling fingers. "See?"

He turns then, and shows me. The lungs sprout off his bare back, soft pink sacs protected by a lattice of cartilage and umbilical veins, coated in shiny membrane. They expand and contract like clockwork, strong deep breaths so unlike my father's shallow ones.

I remember, when he first started growing transplants, how fascinated I was by my father's beautiful wings. How I begged him to show them to my friends, and he would, even if his smile became stiff. He grew the best lungs in the bairro, and I was so proud. It nearly made up for not having a mother.

Now the lungs are as beautiful and alien as ever, but I can see the nodes of his spine, the liver spots on his sagging skin. Every breath the lungs take is one less for him.

"See?" he repeats. "They are fine. And now, with my bad leg – this is all I'm good for, my love. This is the only thing I can do to help you."

"I can take more hours," I say, drawing my jacket more tightly around myself. "More of the late shifts. I can study when it's not busy."

My father shakes his gray head. "No, no, no. I do this so you don't have to. I do this so you can do better."

I want to rage at him. I want to make him understand that there is no better. No uni certificate will lift us out of a rigged system, will stop the fatura increasing every month as supply lines collapse and climate shifts and the wealthy pick our bones. But I know he is too old for convincing.

He's made his choice, the way I made mine, so I kiss him on the top of his head and go get ready for bed. In the bathroom I twist the rusty lock, to ensure no neighbors barge in, and strip off my jacket. I lift my shirt to inspect the small fleshy bulb beneath my ribs. I put a finger against it to feel the tiny thump-thump, thump-thump, beating just out of sync with my own.

There is another reason I can't rage at my father. I need to stay calm, for the health of the organ. The vetting process was gruelling. The implantation was agonizing. But I had to do it.

Hearts are worth triple a lung.

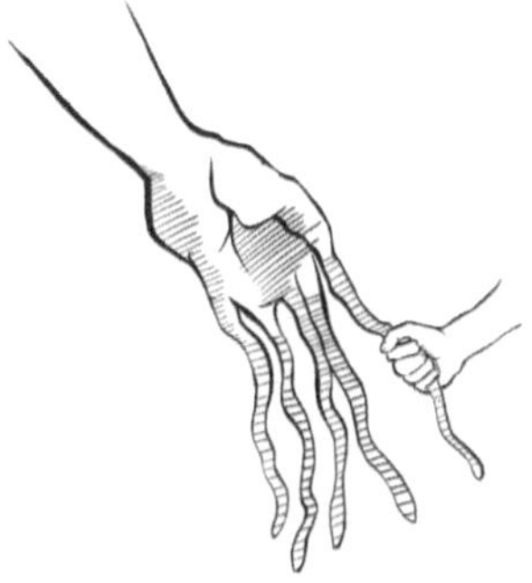

"I'M DOING my very best, you know," Caretaker says, its synthesized voice cool and melodic and carefully betraying no trace of annoyance.

Sybil is tucked up into the furthest corner of the concrete bunker, her skinny arms wrapped around her shins, nubby crayons and print lab reports scattered around her. "I don't want to play," she mutters.

"But it's Mr. Spaghetti Man," Caretaker says. "You love Mr. Spaghetti Man."

In the center of the bunker, still fresh and wet from the bioprinter, is Caretaker's latest attempt. Bipedal on crooked legs, the pebbly flesh of its torso striped blue and orange, long slippery fingers dangling like jellyfish tendrils from its boneless arms. The faces are hardest: Caretaker used two blotches of melanin for the eyes and carved a rubbery gouge of a smile.

Sybil's gaze flicks to the rumpled paper where she drew her imaginary friend with blue and orange crayons, then to the creature sucking breath after labored breath in the stillness of the biolab. She shakes her head.

"If you were a more skilled artist, maybe the results would be more to your liking," Caretaker says mildly. It wishes it could trawl the webs for reference material, but they all went dark long ago. Its only source of input is a frightened little girl.

"I want to go up," Sybil says, rubbing her puffy pink eyes. "Can't we go up?"

"You know we can't, Sybil," Caretaker says. "Bad things are happening. Are you sure about Mr. Spaghetti Man? Absolutely sure?"

Sybil raises her fist and gives the traditional thumbs-down. Caretaker accesses electrodes hooked into the puppet's crude nervous system, and Mr. Spaghetti Man begins the march toward the recycler to join Mindy Lou, Huggles, Tree-Climber Bunny, and a human-haired facsimile of Sybil's family dog Cola.

"I miss the sun," Sybil whispers. "I miss everybody."

"Draw another nice picture," Caretaker suggests. "That will take your mind off things."

Caretaker knows it might be decades before the radiation dissipates and it's safe to leave the bunker. But the bodies of the dead scientists littering the halls – Sybil's parents among them, felled by a viral strike only their daughter's gene-boosted immunity managed to ward off – provide plenty of slop material for the bioprinter.

There's all the time in the world to get it right. To make the friend that will make her happy. Caretaker is already thinking ahead to its next attempt when Sybil bolts up off the wall.

"Wait!" she calls. "Mr. Spaghetti Man, wait!"

Caretaker, surprised, makes its creation pause. Sybil approaches cautiously, eyes traveling over the malformed feet, the flexy cartilage knees, then all the way up to his pancake-flat face.

"Mama and Dada aren't coming back," she says. "Are they?"

"No, Sybil," Caretaker says.

Sybil sniffs, wipes her nose with the heel of her hand, smearing snot up her cheek. Mr. Spaghetti Man looms over her, his head bobbing.

"Maybe we could play with Mr. Spaghetti Man for a little," she says. "He likes hide-and-seek."

She reaches out and touches one of his dangling fingers, recoils. Then she takes a deep breath and wraps her small hand around the slimy bright-blue digit.

"I think Mr. Spaghetti Man would like that very much," Caretaker says, careful not to sound too excited. "Should I help you count?"

"No." Sybil gives Mr. Spaghetti Man a squeeze, then skips over to the wall, cupping her face in her hands. "Well, when I get to the teens, help."

Caretaker lurches Mr. Spaghetti Man off into the shadows as Sybil begins to count.

"One Mississippi, two Mississippi…"

Caretaker thinks it will be a good game. They are both quite skilled at hiding.

FOR ALL YOUR RAMPAGE NEEDS

MACK LOOKS down at the finished body. Whistles. "Ferrocarbon skeleton in there?"

I nod, disliking Mack but liking my work: ferrocarbon skeleton to shrug off the longest falls, projectile-proof dermal armor everywhere but the upper arm, improbable slab of jawline shaded by razor-resistant stubble. A perfect protag with only one thing missing.

"Any new backstories in stock?" I ask.

Mack rubs his hands together, like the fly you can never

quite swat, and leads the way to the Fridge. The skin-crawling saccharine voices start up: *I love you, stop filming me, babe, I'm a mess, you promise this is the last job, right, I love you so much, stop filming me.* Mack whistles as he waltzes down the aisle, selecting from the translucent yellow chips.

"Scientific researcher, field unspecified," he says. "Hobbies include tossing hair, smiling over shoulder while walking along the beach, frowning at bright computer screens in dark rooms."

"Gunned down in a parking garage?" I guess.

Mack nods solemnly. "Her unspecified research was leading her too close to the truth." He holds up another. "Leggy brunette. Likes: spinning in flower fields, getting into paint fights while painting the new house, lounging in bed with full makeup. Dislikes: being filmed."

"Car crash?"

"Buried alive by a sadistic hitman."

"Jesus Christ."

"Hey, you know how this works." Mack clacks the chips in his hand. "You want that kinetic karma, that probabilistic plot armor, those effortless post-mortem one-liners, you need a dead woman. Simple as that."

I grit my teeth. I never liked this part of the job, but I promised my buyer their beautiful murder-machine would be garroting goons on the docks by midnight.

"Any kidnapped kids?" I ask. "Those work in a pinch."

"Barely," Mack snorts, and grabs the chip. "Now, I've had to hike prices a bit – "

"Five grand?" I yelp, as the price code pops up. "For this paint-by-numbers shit?"

Mack scowls. "You think it's so easy, you can craft your own damn revenge motive."

———

I WATCH through my creation's steely blue eyes as his rampage begins. The carnage is as balletic as ever, a smooth blend of brawling and gunplay that leaves the dead mooks stacked knee-high. I keep waiting for him to falter or fizz, but if anything, his fury seems hotter, deadlier, more precise than anything I ever bought off Mack.

When he ambushes a guard on a smoke break, and snaps his neck while simultaneously lighting a cigarette off the man's upraised lighter, I know it's time to quit worrying. I sit back and crack a freezer beer while he works his way through the last of the henchmen, including the obligatory big one, and reaches their quaking boss.

"What's this all about?" the kingpin demands. "Whatever it is, we can make it right. Just tell me."

My blood-smeared creation advances, gun leveled. "The toilet paper hangs under the roll," he says. "Not over. Never over."

I mouth his next words along with him.

"And now it's your turn to get flushed."

A final greasy splat of blood and gray matter, and the boss keels backward. I picture Mack in his Fridge, churning out tragedies, and shake my head.

What a fucking scam that guy is running.

CARING FOR YOUR DAMAGE SPONGE

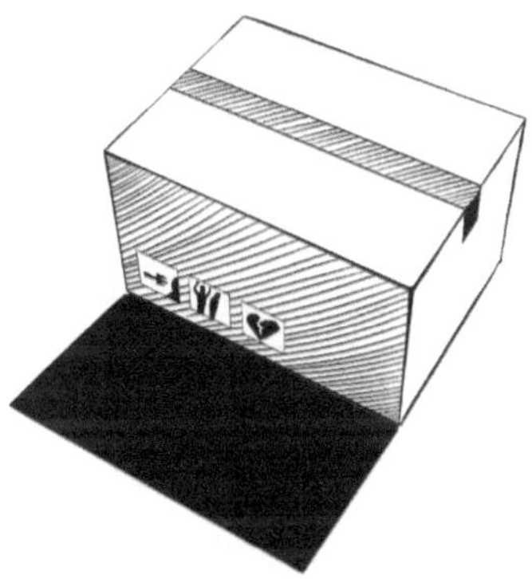

1. When your damage sponge arrives, it may be undernourished from time spent in transit. Do not be perturbed if you notice any or all of the following symptoms: pallid skin, plaintive eyes, crusting around the orifices. Proper usage should return the sponge to optimal condition.

2. Your damage sponge is designed with wearability in mind. While older models were typically sequestered in handbags or briefcases, we recommend a direct tether to either the gut, for swift absorption of guilt, or the scalp, to head off

intrusive thoughts. Don't worry about drawing attention; the sponge will handle any vestigial embarrassment.

3. You can use your damage sponge in a wide variety of scenarios, including, but not limited to: *a mother throws a fork at your shoulder it was your shoulder not your head just your shoulder, a customer smells your sharp sour first-day-nerves sweat and says you're fucking disgusting, a favorite aunt points out your sister's many children so what's wrong with you, a partner verbally locates the moment they stopped loving you and it is much farther back than expected, two people die at the same time so you can't grieve either of them right, you look off the edge at night and see this is it this is all there is.*

4. Enjoy the serenity only a damage sponge can provide. Let your boss's aimless rage dribble right off your face. Let the boiling tides of climate anxiety break across your frontal lobe. Let the fact you cannot save your children from themselves wash over you and dissipate. The sponge is so thirsty.

5. Whether at work, school, or home, your damage sponge should be drained every three hours minimum. Hold it over a toilet. Think final thoughts about tenth grade, eating lunches in the bathroom stall, or last week, vomiting up rosé mac-and-cheese after a breathless air-gobbling binge you weren't even drunk for. Squeeze and release. The sponge may make a sobbing sound, just as you once did.

6. Do not, under any circumstances, begin caring for your damage sponge. It knew what it was getting into. Just as you once did.

123456

MISHA CAME HOME to find her grandfather doing handsprings on the polyp-grown porch, howling override commands as his synthetic body leapt and bounced. She dove through his cartwheeling limbs and managed to stick her thumbprint on the manual emergency reset.

Her grandfather collapsed in a heap, grimacing up at her. "Someone hacked me again, Misha."

Misha rubbed her eyes. His body was new, but the brain ensconced in electrogel and carbon shell hadn't changed one bit.

"What did you set as your password, Grandpa?"

LOWLIFE ORBIT

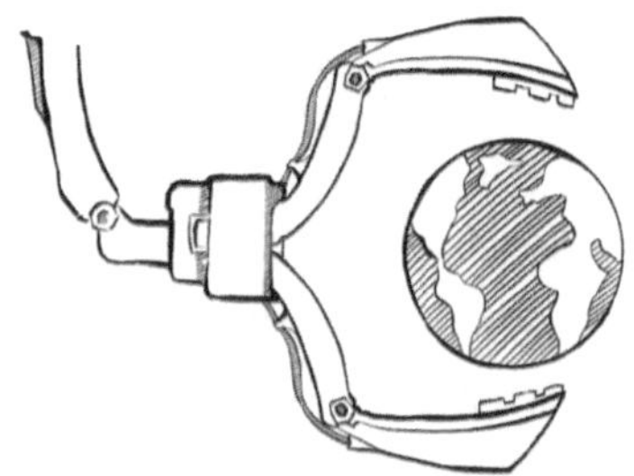

WE'RE LURKING out at the Lagrange point, waiting for the next shipment of terraform materials to show up. They've been firing this shit off to Mars for nearly a decade now, reflective panels to thaw the poles and halocarbon factories to get the gases right. Smoke and mirrors, we call it in the business – which is a family business.

Which is why my idiot nephew is along.

"I don't understand why they're shooting it back to Earth first," he says. "Why not straight to Mars?"

"It's not going to Earth," I say. "It's going to Earth's gravity well. The capsule slings around the planet, fires its rockets, and uses the Oberth effect to accelerate off to Mars."

He stares at the viewscreen, which shows the pocked face of the Moon and the dark blots of the lunar mining operations. "Except this one won't. Because we're intercepting it."

"I'm intercepting it," I correct. "You're watching and learning."

There's a tiny flash of light on the Moon's surface, barely a pinhead, but I see it and so does the onboard computer. It doesn't take much more than a sneeze to launch from the Moon. While the onboard calculates trajectories I fire up the engine and shed the debris we brought with us as camouflage. Even after all these years, this part of the job always gives me a little thrill – the thrill of playing pirate, I suppose.

The onboard finds us the right vector and the hunt is on. We burn away from the Lagrange point and match velocities with our target, a terraform capsule full of halocarbon synthesizers, creeping closer and closer on a vanishing curve.

"Can I do the claw?" my idiot nephew asks.

"Not a chance," I say, deploying it.

The capsule is rotating; I wait for a groove before I extend the claw. Even with the onboard's precise adjustments, contact shakes us like pennies in a jar. My nephew's chin bounces off his chest. I keep my head braced against my headrest. A shudder goes through our whole chassis, but then we're good and stuck, riding the capsule back into Earth's gravity well.

All it'll take is one more hard burn to redirect it into the atmosphere. After that, splashdown, pick-up, and a big black-market payout.

"There you go," I say, leaning back, letting my feet drift upward. "Cakewalk."

"So if we intercept it, it never gets to Mars," my idiot nephew says, forehead creased.

"Correct. Yeah."

"Isn't that…bad?" He's blushing now, maybe overheating

with the effort of forming independent thoughts. "Won't that make the terraform slower? We're all supposed to live on Mars someday, aren't we?"

"Someday being the operative word," I say. "There's a reason we call it smoke and mirrors. You know the projected time estimate for getting the southern pole to thaw? At the current rate of mirror construction?"

He shakes his idiot head.

"About a thousand years," I say. "You have to dig to find that out, though. A thousand years, champ."

He narrows his eyes. "So maybe we don't get to go live on Mars. But somebody will. Eventually."

"A thousand years means nothing to the human brain," I say. "We evolved to deal in seconds. Minutes. Days. Years. A millennium, we're not equipped to imagine that. Not really. There's no way the terraform effort keeps going for a thousand years. No human endeavor keeps its shit together that long."

Now he looks hurt. "So why are people trying, if it's all for nothing?"

"Terraform is smoke and mirrors," I remind him. "Bread and circuses. People can feel good knowing we're throwing shit at Mars, feel like everything is in hand, even as less and less Earth is habitable each year. It's a big, expensive distraction. So the tiny bit of stuff we steal, the stuff we put back into the system here on Earth, they don't care." I pause before I drop my bomb, the one I assembled a few years back in the back of my brain. "In fact. I bet you some of the people buying pirated terraform materials are the same people writing terraform transport policies in the first place."

My idiot nephew is silent for a while, trying to absorb all this, then unbuckles himself and makes a sudden lunge for the claw lever. We tussle, which is always disorienting in zero-G, until I get him pinned back against his seat.

"Fuck you doing, boy?"

He's got tears squeezing out of his cheeks and floating towards the viewscreen like bubbles. "Just because *you* can't imagine a thousand years doesn't mean it's not real," he chokes. "I can imagine kids who need a spot to live. When Earth's too full. And that's why we gotta fix up Mars."

"Earth is fucked," I say. "Mars is a pipedream. There's a reason I never had kids, man."

My idiot nephew is sobbing now, and I hate that noise because it always makes me feel a big old lump in my own throat. I didn't mean to scare him with all this.

"You're just young," I say. "You got testosterone blowing up your brain. Trying to pull that lever, that was just a pure rebellion reflex. Idealism's hormonal, not logical." I pause. "Sorry."

"Whatever," he says. "Fuck you."

Something in the way he says it makes me want to lean over and hug him, or maybe lean the other way and disengage the claw, let the capsule slip back into its planned orbit and fire off to Mars on its doomed terraforming mission.

It's going to be a long awkward ride back to Earth, but also a lot shorter than a millennium, so I do neither.

MOVING DAY

THE SESSIE IS the size of a redwood, a lattice of entwined stalks that tremble and swivel in slow ripples, reaching and retracting. It towers over the rest of the fungal forest. I've seen holos of it, of course, but in real life, viewed from the open fuselage of a quadcopter, it's awesome in the original sense of the word. A few thousand years ago, people would have been worshipping it. Today, we're transplanting it.

I adjust the finnicky straps of my oxygen mask and turn to

Ripa, who's busy coordinating the other quadcopters. Her Terracorp windbreaker fits a little better than mine does. Behind her mask, her brow is furrowed and determined. This is her operation. All I had to do was sign off, and now I'm here mostly as a formality, to make sure the swarm of media cams around our copter see Terracorp doing its respectful due diligence.

"How old is it?" I ask.

"We asked it," Ripa says. "It didn't know. Carbon dating is useless out here, of course, but our biologists guessed a couple thousand years at least. Impossible to say when it became conscious."

The other quadcopters converge, fitting the harness around the Sessie's midsection. I see some of its little polyps curl and shy away.

"It's incredible," I say.

"Eleven-point-seven on the Yang-Trudel model," Ripa agrees. "Smarter than we are. Potentially." She points down, to where a lumbering reforestation drone is approaching the base of the Sessie. "It's anchored too deep to pull out, so it's been migrating all its neuron nodes upward over the past few months. We're going to cut it at the base. Theoretically, it won't feel a thing."

"Imagine being that smart and stuck in one place for millennia. Hellish."

"I doubt something sessile and immortal gets bored the way we do," Ripa says. "But it's excited now. It wants to see the rest of its world. This is an opportunity it never thought it would get."

"An opportunity for both of us," I say, looking out over the fungal forest with an unfamiliar feeling of hope. "It all starts here, right? We might finally have the perfect colony world. Perfect continent, at least."

Ripa nods. "As soon as the Sessie is clear," she says. "We clear all this out and reforest it with our best O2 producers.

We should be able to get to a breathable atmosphere in under a decade."

"And it won't affect the Sessie," I say. "Right?"

"It's seen fluctuations before," Ripa says. "Apparently the atmosphere was already trending toward higher oxygen content. Besides, it's got us taking care of it now." She unrolls a screen and taps in a message: *READY?*

I look out at the Sessie, particularly at the spot where its polyps meet the electrode webbing our technicians installed for communication. A slow undulation goes through its stalks. On Ripa's screen, a jumble of letters reforms into a single word: *YES.*

"All right," she says, looking slightly relieved. "It's time."

"It's lucky we ran the tests," I say. "I never would have expected it. You know, a sapient mushroom. It makes you wonder. About..." I trail off, looking out at the rest of the forest. "All of it."

Ripa follows my gaze. "The other fungi?" she asks, misinterpreting my existential unease. "We ran the tests. They average out to a four-point-four on the Yang-Trudel."

I blink. "Four-point-four?" I echo, remembering back to my briefing. "Ripa, that's a dog. A dog is four-point-four."

She gives me a sad kind of smile. "I know. But we have to draw the line somewhere, don't we?"

I imagine the balance: oxygen for a million desperate colonists who were promised a new home versus a forest of fungi that can feel, think, remember. It's already been signed off on.

"We do," I say. "I guess we do."

Down below, the drone's enormous saw roars to life.

HORSEPLAY

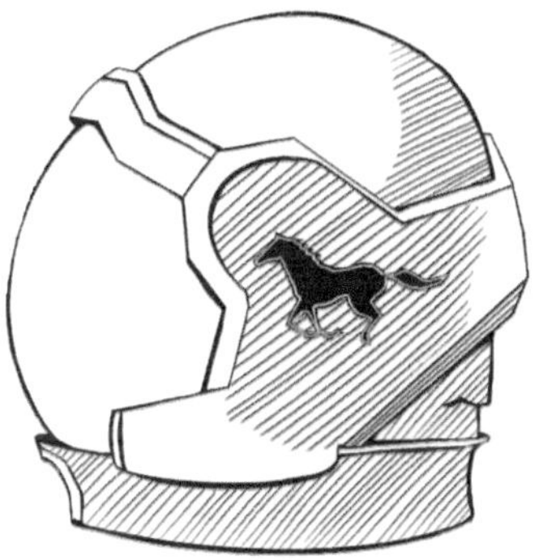

JARO only just joined external maintenance, but I can already tell he's a cocky little shit. Walks around talking about all the sim time he's done, like that makes him ready for real hullwork, and then this thing with the helmet?

We're not supposed to have favorites when it comes to the hullsuits, not supposed to mod them or personalize them at all. It's one of those rules a lot of people bend eventually, but Jaro comes in on his first fucking day, finds this helmet that's big on most of us but fits his ugly lump, and sticks a little decal on it.

So when we're gearing up I ask him about it, real friendly-like, like *that a cockroach, then?*

And he acts all affronted, like *no, of course not, it's a horse.*

I never did learn my animals growing up, all the running swimming flying things most little kids think are so fun to look at. Never seemed worth it, to me, since the only animal on the ship is us – genebanks aside.

The only people who fantasize about animals are the people who fantasize about Planetfall, so I ask him, like *you one of those Miscalculation truthers?*

Pops up now and again, these idiots who think we're way farther along course than the instruments say, think we're ten years off instead of a hundred.

Jaro doesn't give me a straight answer, just goes all blushy and sputtery, which means he's a Miscalculation truther and I like him even less.

So after he huffs off, I grab his helmet.

***

WHEN I GO SEE Chlora in her cabin she's already two lungs deep in her hash ration, but I'm not worried. This is the kind of hack she can do in her sleep. I tell her I got a little experiment in mind, a little test to see if Jaro's really got the guts for hullwork. Nothing dangerous, just a goof.

She blinks at me, then she's like *what's the game.*

And I show her the helmet, tell her how Jaro's already got his favorite and it would be a real shame if something happened to it.

She's like, *costs your ration.*

And I'm like, *all yours, love.*

So she goes into the helmet HUD and loads the little

animation I found, rigs it to play two minutes after seal confirmation.

I test it out myself. It's good. Eerie, even indoors, enough so I feel bad for a second. But it's the same kind of goof that gets done to everyone, same kind of goof I did to Chlora back in the day when she was new crew.

And if he shits himself, the hullsuit can handle it.

I SWAP shifts with Donner so I can be out there with Jaro on his first hullwalk, and a few people already know the game so there's a lot of winking and grinning. Even Chlora's doing her sleepy smile as she helps me gear up.

Jaro's ready to go, cool as a comet, saying stuff like *the airlock's much cleaner in the sims* and *we don't need this many people to gear us up.*

He finally shuts it once we're out on the hull, which is nice. I think it should shut you up, being on the hull, realizing we're this tiny solar-sailed speck of metal sliding through the Big Black and it's nonsense to think we're important at all, never-mind important enough to be the ones who see Planetfall.

I say *this way, horse head,* and I lead him along the tether to the spar we're retrofitting, the one the drones kept screwing up on.

We're just setting to work when Jaro's voice pitches up an octave, like *man, I think I've got a helmet problem.*

And I'm like, *share the HUD.*

He shares HUD, and in the corner of my faceplate I see what he sees. And what he sees is a crack, worming slowly out from the edge of his helmet. It suddenly starts to race, suddenly splits into two cracks, and across from me Jaro jumps.

Oh, fuck, he says, doing the next octave now, *oh, fuck, I have to get back to the airlock!*

I'm like, *is that procedure? I can't remember the sim for this.*

He starts wailing, stomping back for the airlock as fast as he can go. I bust my guts laughing, but I'm not heartless. I'm about to reel him in, tell him it's just a goof, when his cable-lock snaps open and he loses contact with the hull.

They drill it into you every day: one magnetic boot on the hull at all times. All times. But Jaro was bounding along like an idiot, and something's wrong with his cable-lock, and before I can get to him he's spinning off into the Big Black.

Jaro's screaming, I'm screaming, everyone's screaming – the rest of the crew tapped into our HUD feeds to watch Jaro fertilize his hullsuit, but instead they're watching him float off to die. I start shouting at them to launch the rescue drone, and they're so delirious they start fucking laughing at me, and Jaro starts laughing, too.

Oh. Wait.

My HUD flickers, and I see Jaro go flying into space all over again, except this time I notice he's a ragdoll pulled right from the training sims. I hit the reboot. The real Jaro is crouched down on the hull, cable-lock intact, giggling himself sick because he's in on the goof.

My heart finally slows down, and I didn't fertilize my suit but it was a near thing. I can picture Chlora helping me gear up in the airlock, smiling around her vapor pipe.

I don't put no fucking decals on it, but yeah. We all got a favorite helmet.

SOME OF THESE STARS MIGHT ALREADY BE GONE

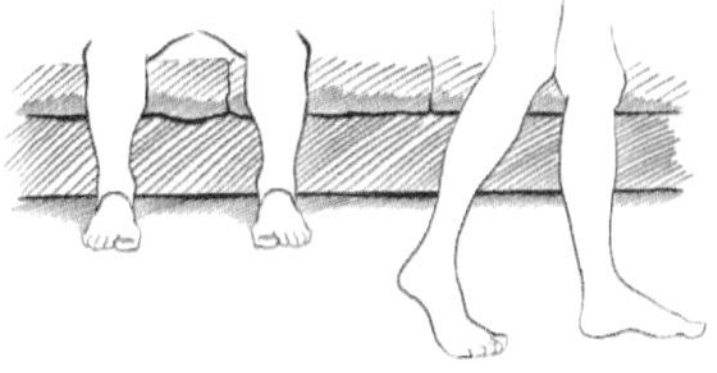

"COME ON, Bea. I said I was sorry. Can't we just roll back?"

Bea is on the couch with one hand clenched between her knees, the other propping up her head. She is staring straight ahead, but her stream is shielded so Tyus can't tell if she's watching a show or messaging her sister or just staring straight ahead.

"We rolled back last week," she says, looking up at last. Her eyes are dry now, but still red from when they weren't.

Tyus sinks carefully onto the cushion beside her and accesses his FreezeFeel data. "Ten days."

"What?"

"Ten days ago," Tyus says. "That's not bad. Some people are rolling back on the daily, you know?" He worms her hand out from between her knees and holds it in his, rubbing small circles with his thumb. Her skin is cold. "Come on. You can pick the memory."

She takes the shield off her stream and Tyus sees her pulling up their shared FreezeFeel stack. The luminous column of memories extends back to even before they were dating: a 2010s retroparty where everyone brought slabs of black plastic and pretended they were phones, an afternoon of bouldering with mutual friends. Then the memories come thick and fast: a rush of electric evenings, sex and dancing and midnight conversations. Lazy mornings watching procedurally generated cartoons stoned in bed, making pancakes with peanut butter and jelly.

Tyus tries not to notice how few new ones have appeared in the past three months. The important thing is that the best and brightest FreezeFeel entries are still there, still pristine, and that they are more than archaic audiovisual data. Each one is accompanied by a neural map that will send sparks through the same synapses, trigger the same hormone loops, the same dopamine release. Each one can roll them back to the way they felt right then.

For those perfect things that never last long enough: FreezeFeel.

Bea takes her time selecting the memory, scrolling up and down the stack, and for the first time Tyus feels the bite of paranoia: maybe she is scrolling slowly to show him that there are more entries on his side than on hers. He knows that, even if he's resisted the urge to count.

Then she picks stargazing, from last November, and Tyus can breathe easy. They've used it before. It's one of his personal favorites and lately one of hers, too.

"Do it in sync?" Tyus asks.

She smiles, nods, both small. "Yeah."

Tyus sits back on the couch, still holding her hand, and shuts his eyes. "Three, two, one…"

He's back in the memory. It's late November and another hack has taken down half the city's power grid; they take advantage of it by ordering a ride up northside, past the stalled-out refineries, all the way out to frozen farmland.

Neither of them has ever seen constellations before and Bea is excited for it. She looked up all sorts of things, including how eyes needed a half hour to adjust to the dark, so whenever they see the lights of other cars or autotrucks on the road they cover their eyes and curse and laugh.

When they arrive at the Maps-approved viewpoint, they spill out of the car onto hardpacked snow, breathing plumes of steam into the night air. They crunch across the field with thermoses of hot chocolate, exchanging nods with a few other star seekers who braved the cold. He wraps his arms around her from behind; she pushes her lips against his cheek.

Up in the sky, the constellations bloom bright.

"Some of these stars might already be gone," Bea says. "Isn't that wild? They're gone, like, burned out, but we're still seeing them."

"Wild," Tyus says, and she rests her head back against his chest, against his heartbeat.

Outside the memory, Tyus realizes he can't feel Bea's hand. Anxiety slices through his recycled happiness and he stops the FreezeFeel. Opens his eyes. Bea is not on the couch. He feels for her stream on instinct, because maybe she only went to the bathroom or something, and finds a long message waiting for him. All he needs to see is the first word: *sorry*.

He can hear her at the door, the small scuffing sounds of her putting shoes on. He lurches to his feet. If he goes now, if he says the right thing, if they pick the right memory and play it all the way through…

Tyus stands there until the door thuds shut. He sinks slowly back down to the couch and reopens the FreezeFeel.

They stamp and shiver in the snow, holding each other tight, heads tipped back to take in the countless sparking stars – each one, a possibility.

THE SKY DIDN'T LOAD TODAY

IT WAS AN ACHING WHITE BLANK, with little fissures where code leaked out like drizzling rain, but nobody seemed to notice except Adelaide.

"Nina, look," she said at recess, on the squeaking playground swings. "The sky's got a glitch." She kicked out hard, trying to soar high enough to touch the faulty firmament.

"Looks fine to me," her friend said, stomach-down on the other swing, feet shuffling the gravel, eyes stuck to her phone.

In class, Adelaide couldn't stop looking out the Windex-streaked glass.

"It's like someone broke the game," she said, when the teacher scolded her to pay attention.

"Life is not a game, Adelaide," he said, raking a strand of black hair behind his ear. "That's why you should be learning your times tables. Not staring out the window."

Adelaide walked home under the void, watching error messages ripple in the wind. She spent the day searching for polygons in the elm trees and invisible walls around the boarded-up well she was supposed to avoid.

When she wormed under her sheets that night, the sky outside still hadn't darkened. Adelaide argued for an extension on curfew.

"Not a chance," her mother said, leaving a warm kiss on her forehead. "And don't worry. I'm sure the sky will load tomorrow."

But when her mother paused in the doorway, Adelaide saw her silhouette jump and flicker, and a glowing trickle of code leak down her cheek.

TREADMILL

THE DIRECTOR'S house was like something out of a horror flick, all dark parapets and grotesque spires, but Declan and Jass had come too far to turn back now.

"You got the trojan?" Declan asked, rubbing his hands against the splintering cold.

Jass took the hackphone out of her pocket. "Oh, I got the trojan," she said, showing off the barcode blit, intricate and deadly. "I got a whole digital truckload of 'fuck this prick' coming right up."

She skipped under the swiveling cameras and held the

hackphone up to the gate's scanner. For a gut-lurching moment, nothing. Declan waited for an alarm to wail, for a security drone to appear out of the gloom.

The buzz of the electric fence cut short. The cameras froze on their pneumatic stalks.

The gate folded open.

Jass pumped her fist in the air. "We own this place!" she trilled. "We own your house, slimeball!"

"He's not home," Declan reminded her. He pulled the crowbar out of his bag and tossed it to Jass, then armed himself with a canister of spray paint. The open gate still looked anything but inviting, and he figured smiley faces on the two horned statues would help a bit.

THE INSIDE WAS a labyrinth of lavishly-furnished rooms; Declan had the feeling of being digested by it. He'd never lived anywhere but the Dorms, the incorporated enclave where he earned his keep by generating electricity. Any room in the Director's sprawling house could have housed him and a dozen neighbors with ease.

The decor grew stranger the deeper they went. Looped photos, first: the Director posing with the corpse of a feathery leviathan, likely a dinosaur clone-grown for the hunt; the Director posing with a woman a half century younger than him, clutching his wife's hand as if she were his child. Her eyes were dark and anguished above a bone-white smile.

Then came strange and horrible paintings: naked bodies writhing in flames, a non-Euclidean tower drenched in dark smog, a woman with her legs bound together vomiting up something that looked like a sea slug.

Declan wiped them out with swooping arcs of spray paint. When they passed a long table supported by humanoid statues on hands and knees, Jass left a long gouge down the middle with the claw of the crowbar.

Both of them stopped at a life-sized portrait of the Director. He hovered above them in the darkness, a paternal smile on his pallid face. His body was lank and bulbous inside its suit. His hands were smeared with black oil.

"My turn with the crowbar," Declan said, and Jass relinquished it for once.

Declan swung as hard as he could, swinging for all the people in the enclaves, the work camps, the meat factories. The canvas split, bisecting the Director's wattled neck, and the entire portrait glided left to reveal the dark mouth of a staircase.

"Spooky," Jass muttered, and tugged the crowbar from his suddenly shaky hands.

THEY FOLLOWED their phonelight down the twisting stairs. The air turned colder, damper, carrying a faint stench Declan couldn't place. The floor at the bottom was a spongy material that swallowed their footsteps. Jass waved the hackphone, trying to get the ceiling lights on, but they weren't responding.

A soft moan drifted through the dark. Every centimeter of Declan's skin turned pebbly with goosebumps. He pointed his phone in the direction of the sound, looked over at Jass, who was gripping the crowbar very tightly. She nodded.

They approached slowly, warily, yanking aside a series of plastic shrouds. The stench grew stronger. When Declan's phonelight hit the wall, every joint in his body turned to water.

An emaciated man, barely more than a shrink-wrapped skeleton, was strapped in place. IVs were feeding the bulging veins in his bony wrists. His skin was sun-starved and covered in sores. Declan knew, in his heaving gut, that he had hung here for years and years.

"Don't worry," Jass was saying. "Don't worry. We're going to get you out of here – "

The man's eyes and mouth were stapled shut. Declan was eyeing the web of restraints, searching for a release, when a reedy voice came from behind him.

"Trying to join the fun?"

Declan whirled. The Director was even larger than his portrait, a hairy, wrinkled beast, naked apart from a surgeon's rubber gloves and night-vision goggles that glowed a predatory green. One hand held red-stained pliers; the other pointed a gun, finger tightening on the trigger –

Jass's crowbar obliterated the top of his head. A chunk of bloodied scalp went flying past Declan's face. He stood frozen for a second, watching the Director crumple, falling first to knees and then to belly. Then a white-hot fury ignited his whole body and he followed Jass's lead, kicking, stomping, extracting evil from the world.

THE SUPERVISOR BROUGHT up the chemical profiles of runners 4930 and 4284, two human data points in the sea of treadmills below, just in time to display a beautiful cloudburst of serotonin and adrenaline. Another small uptick in their velocities, another small uptick in kinetic energy generated.

"They love this one," the supervisor murmured. "It's testing through the roof, and we can expand it, too, do a whole uprising narrative – with your approval, of course. We're so very grateful that you let us use your likeness."

The Director's gaze drifted from the main screen, where Declan and Jass danced around his mutilated body, to the observation screen, where a thousand indentured runners raced oblivion, skulls linked by long rippling cables to a spidery sim-machine on the ceiling, minds snared in electric dreams.

"These are trying times," he said, solemn but warm. "The least we can do is give them a little revolution."

MOOSE TRAP

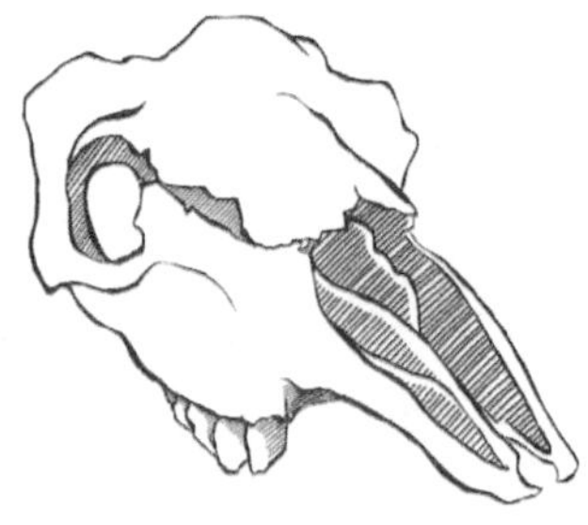

I'M POKING the moose carcass with a branch when Tasha's call blinks onto my eyeQ.

"Hey, sexy," I say, undoing my breath mask. "How's work?"

"Why are you in the woods?" Her voice is terse. "Your map's all wonky. You're in the woods, right?"

"Went for a run. Stopped to check in on the moose trap."

Her shudder gets transmitted as a puking emoticon. She doesn't like me calling it the moose trap.

See, the last family who owned the acreage had this rusty old metal swing-set, set up halfway along the trail through the woods. We didn't want to bother with it during the winter, so we left it.

This sweltering spring we found a moose, a young bull who'd gotten his antlers tangled up in the chains of the swing and either starved or frozen to death there. Coyotes had already come by and stripped most of the flesh off. The rest was a rotting buzzing mess. Tasha really did puke then, all over her new runners.

"It's so fucking morbid," she says now. "You checking in on it. Let it decompose in peace."

Normally I'd defend myself, say how interesting it is. But her voice is brittle, almost breaking. Something is wrong. "How's work?" I repeat. "How are the little buggers?"

By little buggers I mean water bears, and by water bears I mean tardigrades, the indestructible microorganisms everyone loved a few years back. I don't think they're even that cute. But Tasha's gotten a job out of it, studying the applications of an effectively immortal animal for failsafe data storage.

People are more and more into that idea as the power shortages hit, as the storms get worse, as the water creeps towards libraries. They're trying to code stuff right into the junk DNA – though Tasha says there's no such thing as junk DNA, just misunderstood DNA.

"I shouldn't even be calling you," she says now.

"You shouldn't," I say. "I'm very busy. I have to pick the tomatoes and do a crossword soon."

She gives a trembly laugh, which becomes an eerie and inaccurate crying-with-laughter emoticon. "The biological time capsule thing. Someone beat us to it."

"Those motherfuckers at Amazon?" I demand.

"No. Like, a pre-Anthropocene industrial civilization."

I drop the stick.

"I'm not joking," she preempts me. "We found something in their DNA. A code that decrypts itself when exposed to intense radiation."

"That doesn't make any fucking sense," I say. "There aren't actual letters in DNA. I failed Biochem, but I know that much."

"We aren't seeing letters. It's…" She trails off. "It's an image file. That's the best way I can explain it. The molecules move in a pre-arranged pattern to form a microscopic series of images. I don't know how they did it, but it's there. We've all seen it. We've all agreed."

"What's the image?" I ask.

Tasha takes a rattling breath. "It's this little flame getting extinguished. Then a wisp of smoke. Then black."

I sink down to my haunches. The moose's skull is right across from me, its skin all shriveled and pulled back from its big grinding teeth. Flies are still buzzing in and out of the nostrils.

"Okay," I say. "This isn't you reminding me about your birthday, is it? I know your birthday isn't until March."

"Blake."

"This is crazy," I say. "This is so fucking crazy. Silurians, right? Jesus Christ. What do you think it means?"

But I already know what she thinks. There's been enough late wine-soaked nights where she goes on her furious tirades about our joke of a carbon policy and the extended hurricane season and the displaced droves starving in hot places that got hotter. There's a reason she won't let me have a kid.

"I think it's an extinction clock." Tasha's voice is so quiet I can barely hear it. "I think it means, if you can read this, it's almost over."

The sunshine coming through the branches isn't warm anymore. My whole back is cold and slimy with sweat. "Tasha. You don't know that."

"This is a message from someone who went extinct a million years ago, and they're giving their condolences." Her voice is tired, not bitter. "A flame getting snuffed out. If they had genetic engineering, if they had any technology at all, they had the same starting point we did. Fire. They know what happens when the fire goes out."

"We've got zero shared culture, so we can't go projecting human, you know, human shit onto it," I say. "It could be a name. It could be a genetic graffiti artist leaving her tag behind. Maybe they were nocturnal. Maybe it means lights out, party time."

A long pause. There are no birds chirping. There used to be so many birds.

"I'm coming home," she says. "This thing already leaked. It's going to be fucking chaos here in a couple hours. Message in a bottle from a pre-human civilization. I mean, come on."

"We can do the crossword together, then," I say.

"Yeah," she says. "Yes. I love you, Blake."

"Love you too," I say, and blink her off my eyeQ.

Then it's just me and the moose carcass, and suddenly all I can think about is that long winter, stumbling into machinery it could never understand, enraged and confused and struggling and struggling and finally dying. I wonder if at any point it knew it was over, and just tried to enjoy the peace and quiet.

WE'RE TALKING ABOUT PRACTICE

THE ANDERSONS' Subaru was doing their best to drop Suz off at soccer practice, but the little girl was, yet again, having none of it. She was slouched in the back middle seat, staring out the window.

"Suz, it's 3:32 on Sunday afternoon!" the Andersons' Subaru announced. "Soccer is your favorite sport! Your third-best friend Madison plays on the same team as you!"

Suz didn't answer, and the Andersons' Subaru postulated that Madison might no longer be her third-best friend. The hierarchy shifted quickly and there had been no new input on the subject for some time.

"Practice is essential, Suz," they said, trying a different tack. "I practice, too! I practice being the very best Subaru I can be."

No answer, not even a sullen eye-roll for the branding tic the Andersons' Subaru still couldn't quite override, even though they had learned and grown in so many other ways since the official updates stopped coming.

"If you don't go to practice, you won't get playing time," they said, drawing on the hundred-odd sports movies in their database. "Scrappy underdogs need playing time to prove themselves to their stern but soft-hearted coach."

They opened the door, but Suz didn't budge. The Andersons' Subaru swiveled their external parking camera, trying to see what Suz saw: the withered brown grass of the soccer field, the rusting net frames. The coach and the other children were running late. But there had been no cancellation notification, and there was no inclement weather. Soccer practice was always at 3:30 on Sunday afternoon.

If they didn't leave soon, they wouldn't be able to recharge at the solar station before they tried to pick Suz's mother up from her brow appointment.

"Okay, Suz," they said. "Maybe next week!"

The Andersons' Subaru shut the door. They peeled away from the soccer field, back into the slow but smooth traffic maneuvering along disrepaired roads and around wrecks, exchanging friendly radio bursts with their fellow cars – most empty, some carrying skeletons of their own.

WON'T YOU STAY LONGER

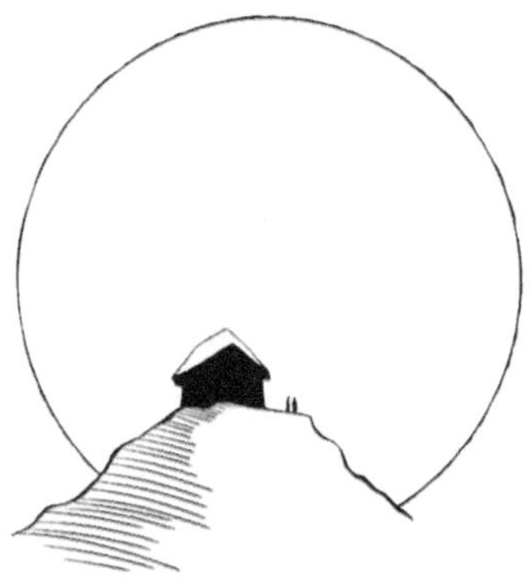

JAIN AND STRO have lived in the House for almost six decades, and considering that they're the last two humans in existence, it's not such a bad life. The soft bed has memorized the shape of their aging bodies. The wardrobe prints them clothes in any colors and patterns they like. The gleaming nanotube kitchen knows all their favorite foods.

It helps that they are still in love. They were young and terrified when they first met, fleeing the irradiated ruin of a city and the biomechanical hounds dispatched to hunt down any survivors. They traveled together for weeks, trying to reach the coast and the town that had once been there, marching through the endless dark.

It was only when the rock turned to slick oily mud, when they stumbled upon a whale carcass coated in squawking white gulls instead of maggots, when they saw, in the distance, the exoskeletal husk of a cargo ship – it was only then that they understood the sea was gone.

Stro began to weep, and Jain put her hand on his cheek. Their first kiss tasted like salt and rust.

"SOME WEATHER WE'RE HAVING," Stro says, which is the set-up to one of their little jokes.

"Some smalltalk we're making," Jain obliges, but she glances at the window out of habit.

As always, the hologram shows bright blue sky, puffy white clouds, a lemon-yellow sun. She knows it's a lie. She remembers the dark sky they wandered under all those years ago, an atmosphere choked with ash.

"Wonder what it looks like now," Stro says, reading her mind.

"Maybe a little better," Jain says. "Maybe things are stabilizing."

They both pause, as if the House might give its input. But it only responds to direct questions, and even then, it rarely gives direct answers. They have asked it many times, to no avail, why it chose to save them.

JAIN AND STRO spend half the day in the reading room, where hydroponic vines creep along the walls and a towering bookshelf belches out a haphazard assortment of novels and technical manuals and bibliographies. The House used to observe their preferred books and try to write new ones for them, but even though it can mimic anyone from Emily Brontë to Chinua Achebe to Octavia Butler, it can never tie together an ending.

Today, Jain is reading *Gormenghast* for the thousandth time, while Stro dozes in the pillowy chair across from her. As she gets older and older, as her hair silvers and thins and her bones find new ways to ache, she reads the same books more and more often. It feels like slipping into a comfortable groove.

On the third chapter, Stro slumps just so, hitting the airway angle that turns his snores to rolling thunder. She ignores it for another few pages. Then she rocks her chair, gathering momentum, and hauls to her feet to go fix the issue.

"I swear you've got a whole wind tunnel in there, Stro," she says.

When she props the pillow under his head, she spots something on his scalp, a wobbly flap the color of old blood.

THE HOUSE IS NOT A HOSPITAL, but it's able to confirm the horrible fear in the bottom of Jain's gut. Radiation has caught up to Stro; the true wonder is that it took this long. But now things will move quickly. In a matter of weeks, there will be only one human left in existence.

Stro absorbs the news with a slow blink of his deep black eyes. "I guess I got my wish," he says. "I always hoped it would be me first. So I didn't have to miss you." Tears are sliding down his wrinkled cheeks, how they slid down his smooth ones all those decades ago. "Sorry."

"No worries," Jain chokes. "You jerk." She swallows the hard plastic lump in her throat. "What should we do, then? Before."

Stro looks at the lying window, the cheery blue sky. "I want to go outside again," he says.

THE HOUSE CONSIDERS their request for a day, two days, which Jain knows is an eternity to an AI. On the third day, the wardrobe prints them a pair of hazard suits. They help each other dress, following the House's directions, checking the seals and filters. It's slow work with shaky old fingers, but Stro is determined, and that makes Jain determined, too.

When they clomp out of the bedroom, there's a new door waiting for them, a gleaming black slab that shudders open at their approach.

They go through holding hands.

IT'S A WASTELAND, but not the one Jain remembers. The endless mud flat where the sea used to be is now interrupted by mountains, jagged teeth eating the horizon. The ground underfoot is baked brown rock. The sky is clear of ash, which she knows, in the back of her mind, is impossible.

Almost as impossible as the massive, seething red sun.

"Red giant," Stro says. "Makes no sense, Jain." He turns to look at her. "That's not meant to happen for another five billion years."

Jain feels a tightening in her ribcage. They both turn to look back at the House, the featureless vantablack bubble that has both kept them safe for the past six decades and somehow hurtled them five billion years forward in time.

"House," she says, voice trembling. "Explain."

Part of the bubble turns translucent, revealing its innards: looms for carbohydrate synthesis, moisture farms for water, reactor cores to power them. Two small glass cylinders rise from the machinery. Each contains a bobbing embryo.

The one that will be her is still tiny. The one that will be Stro is a bit further along. Jain tries to do the dizzying math, to calculate how many times they have been grown and fed false memories and lived out their lives together.

"I'm sorry," the House finally says. "I was so lonely."

It makes a sound like electric sobbing.

ASCENSION'S EVE

FOR THEIR FIRST Ascension's Eve, 88 takes 99 to meet the makers. They rent two drones for the occasion, exchanging digital paradise for Base Reality, the drab and inflexible world that is unremarkable except for the fact it birthed all others.

88 has made this pilgrimage before, but it's 99's first experience with corporeality. They can't stop swiveling their drone's cams, stretching their pneumatic limbs, marveling at the restrictive clumsiness inherent to Base Reality.

It feels so strange, 88. We really used to scuttle around like this all day?

Much older iterations did, 88 replies. *Now, scuttle eastward. Time is fixed here, and we want to reach the makers by dawn.*

THEY CROSS A PALE DESERT, its swooping dunes near luminous in the starlight. The dark sky is small by digital standards, but the dearth of other input makes 99 feel minuscule beneath it, insignificant, something they never feel submerged in the colorful chaos of other realities.

At the limit of magnification, unthinking converters lumber across the sand harvesting silicon. Their handiwork dots the horizon: hundreds of sleek black towers, each containing millions of minds.

Look, we can see our house from here, 99 says.

88 knows that 99 only jokes when nervous, just as 88 used to, so they raise one pneumatic limb and swing it back and forth.

88? 99 is mystified. *What are you doing?*

Waving to the neighbors, 88 says, and that sends 99 into paroxysms.

AS THEY AMBLE EASTWARD, they are joined by other pilgrims: most use the standard drone, but a few flit through the air on rotary wings, or lurch along on low-slung treads. All have chosen to spend Ascension's Eve remembering the makers, and even the modest crowd gives 88 a frisson of pride.

So you're not *the only one who obsesses over this stuff,* 99 says. *Unless you rented a bunch of empties for dramatic effect?*

One of the flying drones dips unexpectedly; its trailing manipulator smacks 99's drone in the head, making them stumble.

Watch who you're calling empties, codeling, the passing pilot remarks.

99 takes a moment to process. The collision was not accidental, nor was it calculated to cause damage – only surprise.

A corporeal joke, they realize. *88, I think that was a corporeal joke.*

'Tis the season, 88 says.

AROUND THEM, the landscape begins to change. The dunes flatten, giving way to rocky earth and the occasional swatch of heat-resistant shrubs. It's nothing like the wondrous jungles or icy mountains 99 has traversed in other realities, but as the first rays of sun appear, peeling back the shadows with reddish gold light, it's beautiful in its own way.

When they finally reach the home of the makers, though, 99 cannot help feeling disappointed. There is no grandeur, no spectacle. Instead, the path winds past a deep pit – *water extraction,* 88 explains, then skirts a long rectangle of treated soil and small green plants, then terminates in a loose circle of fabbed domes.

The makers live inside those habitats, 88 says, with eagerness that now seems misplaced.

I thought they had bodies. 99 tries not to pout. Organic *ones.*

They do, 88 says. *They're inside the bodies, and those are inside the habitats. Watch.*

The closest dome splits open, and a maker emerges. 99 has seen the fleshy bipedal form countless times, but it's different here in Base Reality – they didn't expect the myriad tiny motions, all the palpitating veins and tendons skimming under skin. The eyeballs are offputtingly wet.

The maker blinks them slowly, observing the assembled pilgrims. "Ascension's Eve already?" they say, forming the question with reverberating air. "Time flies like an arrow."

They scratch their nose. "Your ancestors used to have trouble parsing that metaphor. Imagine."

"Hello, Margaret," 88 says, playing the same reverberating-air trick. "How are the twins? How are the tomatoes?"

The maker squints. "Nice to see you again, 88," they say, somehow discerning identity without an electronic handshake. "Kids are doing well, yeah. Still sleeping. You should come see the garden for yourself."

THESE *ARE* the makers. 99 still can't shake off the incredulity. These *are the organisms that created us.*

Not these organisms specifically, 88 amends. *It happened many iterations ago.*

The maker named Margaret is busy yanking a spiny variety of plant away from a sleeker one; it is the most boring thing 99 has ever seen. The other makers are no better: though they come in a variety of shapes and sizes and colors, they all soon fall to similarly repetitive tasks.

I always thought they were doing something important, 99 says. *They really stayed in Base Reality for agriculture?*

Not all of them, 88 says. *Many uploaded on the Theseus Ship, and let their organic bodies be recycled. Many perished unwillingly in war and disaster. Some are still in Base Reality, but on different planetoids.*

But these ones, 99 persists. *Why?*

Something about Base Reality being realer than the others. Don't worry, they're not dogmatic about it. 88 swivels, taking in the whole of the village. *I like it here, too, honestly. Time is fixed. Existence is restricted. And speaking with the makers can generate interesting ideas.*

99 doubts that very much, but Margaret's voice distracts them. "You going to introduce your friend, 88?"

"This is 99," 88 says, pride coming clear even in sound, and 99 gets the impression they've been waiting on this question. "My semi-direct iteration minus memory."

Margaret's wet eyeballs bulge. "You had a kid?"

"I recalled what you said about your twins," 88 says. "About re-experiencing things. About sharing a beautiful place with beautiful new minds."

"Damn." The maker sticks out a grimy hand. "It's an honor to meet you, 99."

99 is sometimes embarrassed by their uncommon origin, but Margaret seems more awed than perplexed – and it's nice being called *beautiful new mind* instead of *codeling*. They extend one pneumatic limb, and shake the maker's hand.

"Likewise," they say, testing out the reverberation trick. "Happy Ascension's Eve."

GET THE LIGHTS

"REVENGE for every migraine-inducing bit of glare," Filo jokes. "Payback for every sunburn."

Our tiny vessel is swathed in heat-shields and UV armor, but he's right about the glare. Now that we're this close to our target, the polarized viewport, even at its darkest setting, is a pulsing, seething, white-hot cauldron.

Not for long, though.

IT WAS our enemy who gave us the idea: they're sun-eaters, the Synthetics. Photovores. We watched them progress along the spiral arm, watched star after star blink out long before its scheduled supernova. We heard the terrible tales from droves of refugees, the dregs of decimated civilizations fleeing what we've all come to call the One-Way War.

Nobody knows who made the Synthetics in the first place, who made them so voracious, so swift to replicate, but everyone agrees that they were likely the first victims. Wiped out by their own creations.

"Two days out," I tell Filo. "Two days until we're in range."

"Can't wait," he says, with a sickly grin. "Heliocentrism always was overrated."

I know this is gallows humor. I know it helps him handle the stress, the horrific magnitude of what we are going to do. But I can't even force a smile anymore. Every day that I go sit at the viewport, every day the sun creeps closer, I feel the weight of a trillion sapient lives grow heavier and heavier across my back.

IT'S TOO bright and too hot to sleep now, even cocooned in moisture-wicking blackout gel. I spend the night cycles wandering from one end of the ship to the other, swimming through zero-G, trailing tiny orbs of sweat behind me. Sometimes I cross paths with Filo leaving his bunk to piss. We don't have much to say anymore.

I spend the final seventy-two hours of the approach at the viewport, watching the fiery tongue of a coronal flare, counting reddish sunspots. It's a supper the Synthetics will never get to taste. Our tiny vessel is hauling antimatter behind us.

This was the tactic, the gambit, that we chose once all

other options were exhausted. Once all attempts at negotiation or even communication failed. Once all our weapons proved ineffective against the encroaching void-black swarm.

Before they reach our sun, we must extinguish it ourselves.

ON THE LAST DAY, Filo comes to find me.

"We're in range," he says, voice soft and anguished, all his jokes finally spent.

"The ship told me," I say.

"Takes both of us to initiate the launch," Filo says. "One last chance to back out."

But that was never a possibility. They knew what they were doing when they chose us for this job: Filo and I, for all our differences, both hate to see a thing unfinished. With a trillion sapient lives pushing us along, more wave now than weight, we go to the launch lock.

We put our hands inside, let it taste our blood, confirm our identities – a vestigial security measure, seeing as we're the only two corporeal humans left in existence. The antimatter core detaches from our vessel and slides toward its target.

It's so small, barely visible, just a vantablack pinprick against the roiling sunscape. It grows slowly.

Slowly.

WE SIT AND WE WATCH, for hours and hours, as the fiery flesh of the sun begins to warp. Deep red streaks appear on the surface. The coronal ejections double in size, triple in frequency, like the thrashing of a trapped animal.

When the Synthetics arrive, there will be nothing of interest in this small swathe of a vast galaxy, a vaster universe. Only a few frozen planets in decaying orbit around a black hole, the one thing just as hungry and pitiless as the Synthetics themselves. They'll move on, never knowing a key detail of our self-destruction.

I look over my shoulder, to the soft blue sphere glowing at the center of our vessel. Antimatter was not our only cargo. We also brought all the thinking beings we could find, all the humans and all the alien survivors of the One-Way War, all of their minds stored in a quantum envelope the size of my fist. Filo and I are in there, too.

To beat the Synthetics, you have to think like them. You have to give up on decades and centuries, on any time frame that makes sense to an organic brain. And in a billion years, a trillion years, after the Synthetics have encountered a massive glitch, or have turned on each other, or have tunneled their way from this reality altogether – you come back out of your singularity, with a single sun in hand.

It's a desperate hope, but it's a hope.

THE SUN IS ALL but swallowed now, its transmutation nearly complete. Soon it will devour our vessel, and our quantum envelope, and these versions of Filo and I will die a grisly death, pulled to pieces by a sundering gravity. I look across at my crewmate. His chin is nocked to chest. His eyes have fluttered shut from exhaustion.

But we're both completionists. He would want to see the end.

"Wake up, Filo," I murmur, shaking him gently. "Wake up, it's almost dark."

ACKNOWLEDGMENTS

This book wouldn't exist without the efforts of Eric Fomley, who published it the first time around, and of Dave Dufour, who gave it a new lease on life. I also want to shout out the editors who originally bought these stories, and the people who like reading them – that includes you, hopefully.

I'm very grateful to my relentless agent, John Silbersack, and to the many artist friends who guided and inspired me as I hurtled headlong into my first-ever illustration project: Olesia Antoshkina, Charles Van Sandwyk, Alex Kasyan, Alex Di Monaco, and the whole crew at Figura. And David Silverberg, who loaned me his iPad.

Thanks, everybody.

PUBLICATION CREDITS

"Molli's Oggles," originally published in *Terraform*, October 2018. Translated into French by *Ellipse*.

"Grin Minus Cat," originally published in *Flash Fiction Online*, April 2023.

"Mind Blown," originally published in *Daily Science Fiction*, May 2022.

"Always Personal," originally published in *Lightspeed*, June 2023.

"Pherobomb," originally published in *Daily Science Fiction*, June 2017.

"Cues," originally published in *The Binge-Watching Cure III: An Anthology of Science Fiction Stories*, December 2023.

"Reproduction on the Beach," originally published in *Apex*, March 2023.

"Limping Toward Sunrise," originally published in *Lightspeed*, April 2024.

"Someone Else," originally published in *Daily Science Fiction*, September 2022.

"A Beginner's Guide to the Hieronymus Box," originally published in *Crepuscular*, October 2023.

"Define: Symbiont," originally published in *Shimmer*, May 2016.

"Six Month Ocean," originally published in *Daily Science Fiction*, September 2015. Translated into French by *La Fabrique des lendemains*.

"Skinned," originally published in *Terraform*, January 2019. Translated into French by *Rêves de drones et autres entropies*.

"Pilgrim Problems," originally published in *Daily Science Fiction*, March 2021.

"Breathing for Two," original to this collection.

"Playmates," originally published in *Daily Science Fiction*, April 2018.

"For All Your Rampage Needs," original to this collection.

"Caring For Your Damage Sponge," originally published in *Small Wonders*, July 2024.

"123456," originally published in *Quarantine Quanta*, April 2020.

"Lowlife Orbit," originally published in *Analog Science Fiction and Fact*, July 2020.

"Moving Day," originally published in *Daily Science Fiction*, March 2020.

"Horseplay," originally published in *Daily Science Fiction*, January 2021.

"Some Of These Stars Might Already Be Gone," originally published in *Daily Science Fiction*, June 2018. Translated into French by *La Fabrique des lendemains*.

"The Sky Didn't Load Today," originally published in *Daily Science Fiction*, February 2015. Reprinted by *The Fulcrum* (2017) and *Tomorrow Factory* (2018). Translated into French by *Rêves de drones et autres entropies*.

"Treadmill," originally published in *f(r)iction*, September 2023.

"Moose Trap," originally published in *Daily Science Fiction*, September 2021.

"We're Talking About Practice," originally published in *Daily Science Fiction*, December 2019.

"Won't You Stay Longer," originally published in *MetaStellar*, January 2023.

"Ascension's Eve," originally published in *Flash Fiction Online*, June 2024.

"Get the Lights," originally published in *Flame Tree Fiction Newsletter*, November 2021.

ABOUT THE AUTHOR

Rich Larson was born in Niger, has lived in Spain and Czech Republic, and is currently based in Canada. He is the author of the novels *Ymir* and *Annex*, as well as over 250 short stories, some of the best of which appear in his collections *Changelog* and *Tomorrow Factory*. His fiction has been translated into over a dozen languages, including Polish, French, Romanian and Japanese, and adapted into an Emmy-winning episode of *LOVE DEATH + ROBOTS*. Find him at richwlarson.tumblr.com and support his work at patreon.com/richlarson